The Va

by

R L Southgate

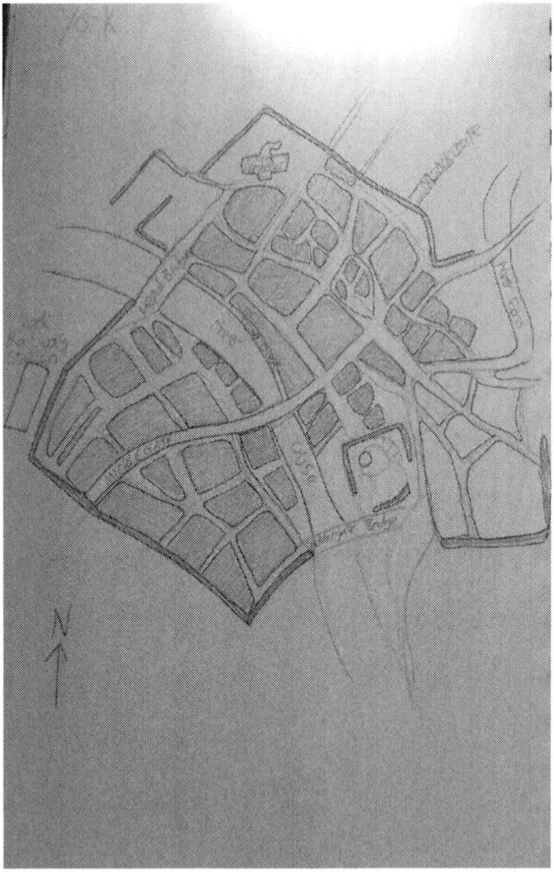
Ouse
N

2

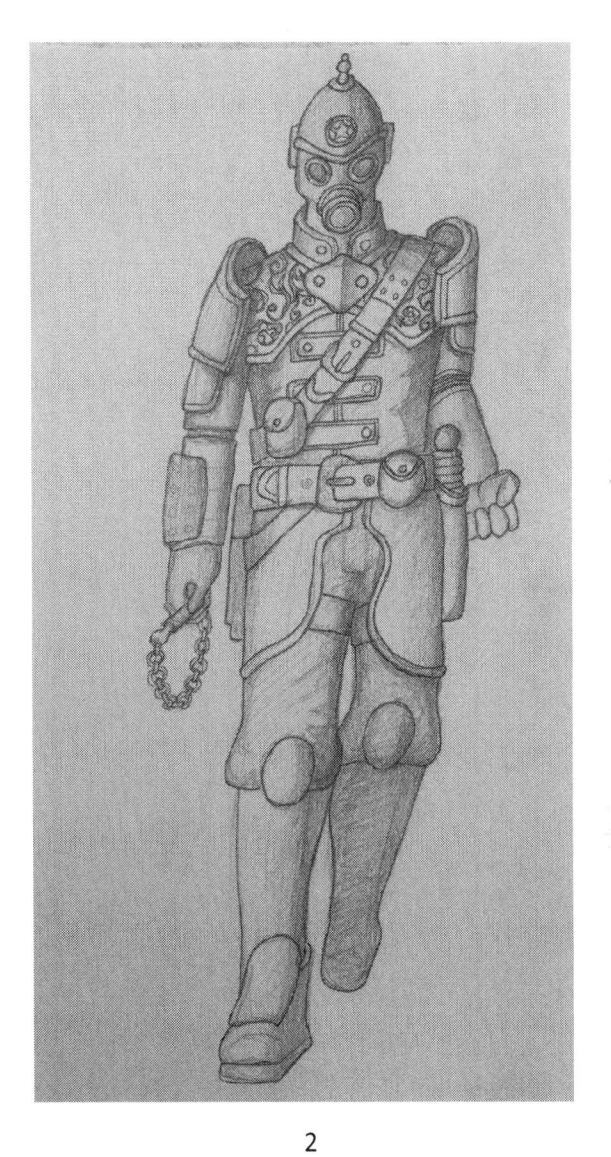

Chapter 1

The smog was thick that night and it was cold too. The constable walked slowly along the dock between Lendal Bridge and Ouse Bridge then would cross over and back down the riverside walk, then would move further down to Skeldergate Bridge and the old prison, then repeat, it was like this most nights, the same old boring beat, his mind would begin to wonder, like why was he doing this, it had become a thankless mind numbing job, the pay was low, but knew he had to start at the bottom and work his way up, prove his peers wrong, but just lately there had been break ins, machinery broken or sabotaged, there was always those who hated progress and this industrial revolution had brought that right out especially when they came, the Fair Ones as they were known but with them came resentment , they brought technology but with it trouble now Adam was not bothered they seemed harmless enough but of late the police force were spread very thin, always on calls, logging complaints there was a rise in crime, murders and disappearances.

Adam Watts shivered in his black woollen long coat and standard black uniform with its shiny buttons down the front truncheon at his hip, tall black helmet and shiny badge on the front and he wore it with pride not that his father would ever approve having not followed in his footsteps not wanting to be an inventor but to help people and make a difference, it was not that his father did not, and was a great man he had done great things there would be not trains or steam power the way it was but would have not got this far without Fair Ones but Adam wanted to see justice, the world was changing fast now and with it crime followed, the system was stuck in the past and that had to change too.

He breathed on his cold hands peering through the mist seeing shapes and swirls made it difficult to see, the light of his lamp glared back at him he had good hearing and so relied upon it, that and his Sharpe instincts, and attention for details, been a constable was not at all glamorous, people even hated them, he did not chase robbers or anything like that it was mostly the drunk or prostitutes and disturbance of the peace, they would spend the night in a cell and be back out again those that were vagrants it was a warm bed for the night mostly he would move them along, it was not dangerous work if they saw the suit coming they would go, some might give him some lip but would move along without much more trouble than that, so after five years on the force he was not afraid, he was tall and quite an imposing figure with blue eyes and black hair with a fare few admires, the ladies liked the uniform this made him smile it was what gets him through these cold nights some nights nothing happened at all.

This night started like any other but was unusually quiet then he heard breaking glass then a scream he ran along Kings Staith in the direction it came from, it was crunchy under foot but it was not glass but some bug shell nothing like he had seen, but since the Fair Ones came there had been a lot of strange things going on. He arrived there was a body on the floor it was a young woman a door was hanging of its hinge, he bent down close to see if she was dead but pulled back what he saw disturbed him, he had seen a dead body before but this was different, the look on her face was sheer terror and fear like something had

been sucked out of her, mouth open in a
silent scream now, eyes wide and staring
her body ridged and stiff which was strange
she had not been dead that long merely
minutes maybe not even hours like it would
suggest he called out for assistance and
blew his whistle.

He stayed with the body but nobody came
he blow on the whistle again still nothing,
he waited for what seemed like forever
there was only one thing that came to mind
so he picked up the body and carried it on
his shoulder in a fireman's lift style back to
the station she was light there was nobody
around at 2am and he wished he was in bed
rather than carry a dead body through the
great city of York and it was called that for a
reason, it had been the capital of England
and now remained so it had grown along
with the industry it had grown out of its
walls with the need for more homes and
factories that were huge with chimney
stacks dominated the skyline even standing

over the minster it to had grown and expanded now York already had enough pubs and if you did not know where they were then you would get lost because if directions were needed these were the landmarks that were used and so even more had popped up to and he passed a few on his way it was a small station near the massive train station he just hoped there would be at least one officer there he was in luck as he burst in surprising the sergeant behind the desk who now looked half asleep which quickly changed when he saw a constable carrying a dead body he too saw the frozen face of fear and almost spilt his coffee.

"Take that away; get it down stairs with the others".

The sergeant said offering no help so Adam Watts had to carry on holding her they had a small cellar where such things as body would be stored for a short time it was a small room there were two more body's under sheet the room smelt bad a kind of sickly sweet smell he breathed through his mouth and laid her down and covered her the same it was strange for there to be so many down here it was a very rare thing in deed so out of curiosity he looked under the sheets and saw the same frozen in fear face's as the prostitute he had brought in, they may be considered low life and scum but they were still people he thought, life and most of the time those that complained about the back alley whores were the people that went there themselves. Adam Watts went back upstairs to fill in a report the smell seemed to cling to him though and was given a fowl look from the sergeant.

"So this as happened before. Why has it been sent up to the City Marshal".

Adam Watts said.

"People die all the time".

The Sergeant said and did not seem to care less.

"Yes, but three the same way. It's murder and needs looking into".

Adam Watts said.

"It has nothing to do with you constable, you still have time left on your shift, it will be dealt with".

The sergeant said, he was fat and had not liked him since he started there, always giving him the worst areas and shifts and seemed to resent his newness and enthusiasm or him rocking the boat and the man's steady desk job, causing more paperwork and making him work for once.

Adam Watts walked his beat nothing else happened that night but he was angry at himself for not standing up to him and frustrated at always been held back and told to get on with his work and not ask questions he could not just simply keep his head down like everybody else it was not in his nature, but he was just a constable and they would soon drop him back down to citizen so his hands were tied but that did not mean he would not leave it this was not just some random murder and definitely not naturel.

Adam Watts finished his shift but that uneasy feeling did not leave him or the smell. He did not sleep well that day and was tired when it came round to his night shift again when he went in the sergeant was in his usual foul mood and most likely made worse by the fact the City Marshal was there which meant he would have to do some actual work, the Marshal wanted to speak with Adam Watts he was a stout man with a large moustache and looked like he had just stepped out of a safari all that was missing was a Pif hat and a rifle. It was unusual for a Marshal to visit let alone one who want to talk to just a constable he took him into one of the small side offices and questioned him about that night but there was nothing new to tell or anymore that was on his report.
"Have there been others sir, with the same rigger and that face".

Adam Watts said.

"It is no concern of yours, and better left to us, you are not to pursue this case anymore".

The Marshal said and meant what he said.

"So it is a case then, so if there has been more, you would know how they died, they were far too stiff for the time of death".

Adam Watts said meaning to push the man to see his reaction which was anger.

"You will not speak of this matter to anybody else, if you are found in any way connected to this you will find yourself without a job, do you understand".

The Marshal said his face turning a little red the man was in his late forties but still looked strong maybe a touch overweight.

"I understand sir".

Adam Watts said but it just made him even more curious and to threaten him to stay away with that said the man left. He went to see where his shift would be for the night it was not the docks but an industrial site on the outskirts of the city away from the case he thought, he nodded and took it without a word for now he would keep a low profile but he was not about to give up on it , they were hiding something especially with the city marshal's involvement which would only mean one thing, it was big and with them coming to him said a whole lot to him, the man had almost seemed afraid even.

2

Lady Duchess Sarah Newcomen had not set foot out of her home in months in fact nothing would get her out there and she did not care what people thought about her and gossiped behind her back, they did not see what she could. Sarah Newcomen knew she was not crazy and had learned from an early age not to tell anybody about what she could see. It was the Fair Ones, now many were beautiful some tall and regale others small all with their pointy little ears and of cause what they had done that had turned a dying land of just farms up to a

thriving and advanced people so of course
all sang their praises, so for her to see
something more, past their lovely façade
and see evil walk among them unseen and
they were everywhere they did not know
she could see them this way and that was
how she wanted it to stay, then there was
the bugs that nobody seemed to see, so she
stayed inside to avoid the demons her skin
pale dark circles around her eyes she did
not sleep well either she was all skin and
bone everyone kept telling her to eat and
get some sun on her skin and get married,
these were all the things she was supposed
to be doing but she was very headstrong
and stubborn not in a bad way mind but
knew what she wanted and that tended to
scare men away they wanted their little
house

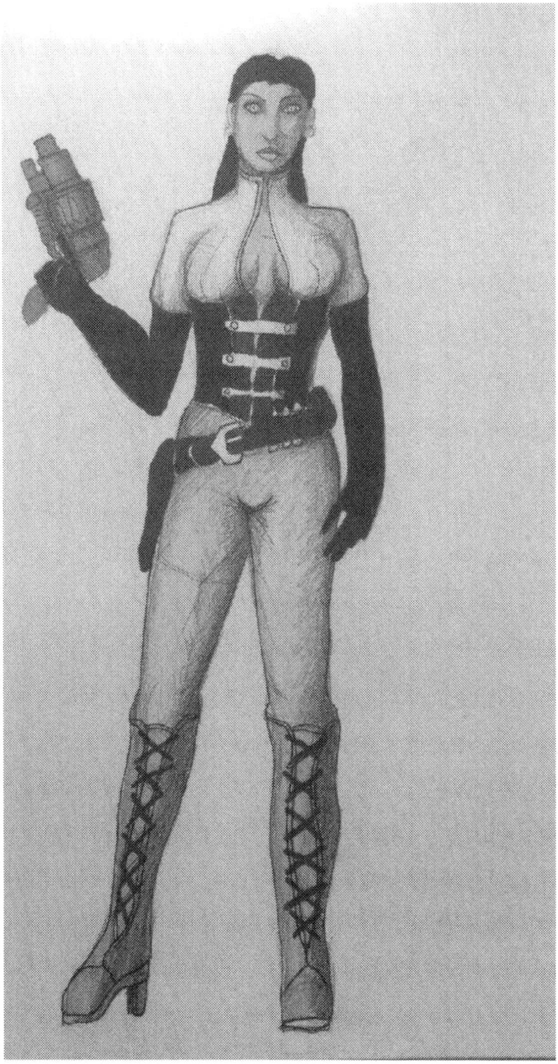

wife's this was just not Sarah Newcomen, she remembered her first sight of them and it played over and over in her mind since, they were thin and emaciated skeletal features big mouths full of teeth and a second pare further in the mouth long arms ending in terrible claw like nails but to everybody else they were just a tall fairy and so of course been a young girl who pointed and screamed nobody would believe her she had therapy and a visit to the insane asylum with its smelt of urine with screams in the night had soon turned her into a great liar she no longer screamed and pointed keeping it to herself and so they called her the crazy Duchess behind her back if it was not for her mother she had been a formidable woman they would of locked her away her passing had hit Sarah Newcomen hard even though she had not believed her she had stood by her she was on her own now there was only so much pretending she could do but nobody would believe her but keeping it all in was taking its toll and if any did she would never see the light of day not that she did anyway but she could ruin everything but not all were like them and where they even aware of them too, so she was stuck or maybe the Fair Ones could help her but she would have to step outside just thinking about it made her pulse race and stomach knot even a knock at the door would scare her let alone answering it.

Sarah Newcomen was not short of money with the title to go with it and she did long to have the life of a normal lady with their fake laughter and big dresses but they were shallow looking down on others thinking themselves superior they made her sick and no better than the demons she saw but they were that evil on the inside but that did not stop her seeing through them too. So her only outlet was shooting and was a damn good shot too, even the bow in her early years she would go shooting with father and she would beat all the men and boys every time they thought it was cute, she thought about their faces on the targets but her mother's passing had hit him hard too, so he hit the bottle harder people would stop coming round after he told them to shove off and lot worse words than that so he drank their money away while she hid away. And when she did dare a look there seemed more of them closing in but nobody could see the danger and they would look at her as if knowing she knew but like her they too did not want to blow their cover any more than she did, it was frustrating and as the months become years she knew something had to be done but her own anxiety grow and hated how it made her feel she would have good days where she had almost stepped out the door even the back yard door was hard, other days she would just stay in bed and told the servants to leave her alone, they too were worried for her she only kept one woman now she was a lot older than her and had been with the family for years and was the closest thing to a mother with a sweet Scottish accent called Mary, now she would fuss over her too, wanting to fetch the doctor she meant well and all but it would not help, she wanted to reach out to one of the Fair Ones, maybe they would believe her, somebody had to or she was going to commit herself to some electric shock treatment or blind herself, other darker thoughts had gone through her mind to end it all but something deep inside held her back told her to be strong and it was not the way, some days those dark days she would stare out the window wondering what it would be like to fly through the air, then she would shake her head and told herself to be strong and not be foolish like some heartbroken girl, now of course she did want to find love and longed to be loved, somebody to share her life with and do all those things, but who would have her she thought with all that was going on she felt something was coming, an uneasy feeling in the pit of her stomach that things were going to get worse and time was running out she had to break free of the house that was more like a prison every day.

Sarah Newcomen felt in a lighter mood this day her mind clear for once and so called Mary to her.
"I want to talk with the head or leader of the fair Ones, will you send a letter I don't know who to send it to though".
Sarah Newcomen said.
"I will find out for you my ladyship right away, I think I know of one that might be able to help, she helps out with the poor and ill her kind and ours".
Mary said with a smile and a glance she did a little bow and scurried away it would give her something to do instead of fussing over her, a purpose would do her good and out

of her hair, so if they did believe her and not carting her off, then what she just hoped the one that received it was not one of them. Her letter was very vague and seeming only work related this was big and would affect all if she was right.

*

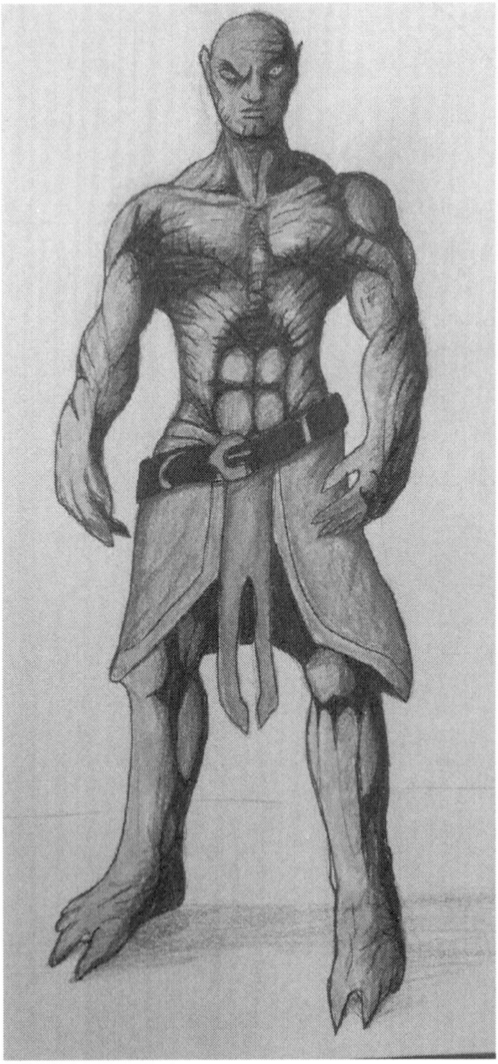

The dweller looked over the sprawling city that seemed to grow every day an unrelenting never sleeping beast, relentlessly bellowing and belching smoke out, he felt free up here among the chimneys and rooftops, it was like another world nobody bothered him up here, people just did not seem to look up or care what was above them. On the odd occasion he might help them, somebody been attacked at night or robbed, he would drop down and help but be gone again unseen, he felt sorry for them working all day and night then doing the same the next day over and over, he watched the world change since they came, the Fair Ones bringing with them the noise and pollution machines of steam, smoke, iron and metal. Factories of brick and metal, rose of homes for the workers their children playing in the narrow streets washing lines sheets flapping above them with their rings of metal and skipping ropes and other such games and the circle would go on he moved across the rooftops jumping gaps and climbing he could move fast and silent.

It was getting late, the smog was rising and those that prowled the streets would walk free, walking tall and unseen but pure evil, how could these thing not be seen he thought they too had come with the Fair Ones could they not see them either, he made his way to the Minsters highest tower, there was a break in the shutter that kept the pigeons out, here was his home and the higher the better he felt at home in this ancient place with its gargoyles and architecture, and as for the pigeons they were on his menu today sometimes he might throw in a rat or a cat if he was quick enough, then there was the trash bins at the back of food shops or restaurants, they would throw away good stuff some even fresh but if he was seen or spotted they would run in fear of his features, his pale skin they would whisper about an urban legend saying they would steal them away in the night if they did not sleep or be nice but it was not true, the truth was he pitted them but was blamed none the less, the evil that walked the streets were to blame not him, in the days he helped them the more they found him with blood on his hands and after trying to save a man too, but it ended up looking like he had done it, they had been so quick to place blame on what they feared and did not understand, he did not look like them, his body had adapted to his way of life, strong, fast and agile.

Something was growing an approaching darkness, he felt it in his bones right to his core more people were going missing, machinery broken and sabotaged, the constables were short on men and losing the battle for the streets those higher turning a blind eye to it all he could almost smell the corruption in the air and the fear too, and strange bugs would also come, they crawled all over they too were unseen but not to him, he would sleep but the horrors would lie in wait there too, crawling through his nightmares and then he would wake covered in sweat, shaking and in tears then he would run and jump to clear his mind for the day, there was one place he could go and that was to see the woman in her garden, some days she would stand in the doorway, he would watch her from afar she was beautiful but would run from him in fear at seeing him approach with his features, he was no gentlemen that would caught her with their fine clothes and money he meant her no harm and felt bad for watching her like that, she made his heart flutter and long to hold her but it would never work, they were too different, his love was of her not for power or some shallow way like those other men and so called lords looking down on the poor and less fortunate, he wanted to take her away from it all but what could he offer her though he thought. He had no home, wealth or land he know something was coming and all were going to suffer, then on that day they would not run from him, they would need him for what was coming and it was going to be far worse but who could he warn or tell or turn to, he could not sit and watch from afar but he felt helpless they would lock him away and run in fear from him when all he had done was help and guard them even though they hated him, he would still save them if he had to, even the fair Ones and they too had been met with hate when they had first come to the city, it had been a lot smaller back then but progress had to come they had helped the economy taking the people out of a dark age but it too had a dark price. He moved on watching the lives below him going on about their own business unaware of him their protector but the time would come he thought.

It was getting dark and starting to rain when he set off back to his night roost when he heard gun fire and a shout he quickly used his speed and parlour skill to where the sound was coming from, jumping impossible gaps landing with a perfect roll and was soon there, below him was a stocky man dressed in metal wearing goggles and what he faced was one of the night stockers, its long arms that ended in claws kept him back but he had already injured it but was cornered his armour would not last much longer how was this man seeing the demon he was not one of the Fair ones, either way it was a good sign if there were others fighting them then there was hope. He dropped to the pavement in silence, waiting for his moment to strike and save this one if there was more than they should join so saving one might help the man who was on the ground now, the demon was about to deliver a final blow the dweller stepped in and kicked it aside and stood between the man and demon it turned and stopped in its tracks and looked him up and down unsure of what it faced or what to do.

"You can no longer hide there are those that can see through your Vale now, run back to whatever hole you crawled out of or face me".
The dweller said to the demon, but his touch had awoken something inside him, images flash into his mind this creature before him seemed familiar like he had face their kind before, then another image popped in there, it was him looking down at his hands and they were human, then it was all gone again it was just him facing and the demon who hesitated, the man was back up now, outnumbered it ran back into the shadows the man thanked him but was confused at what now faced him.
"You have nothing to fear from me, how is it you can see them".
The dweller asked him he held up his goggles with tinted lenses.
"Father made them so we can see them, you are the Dweller".
He said looking a little nervous
"I wish to see your father".

The dweller said.

"Yes we can arrange this but he is not my father, it's what we call him, he is our leader and saviour like god himself sent him to stop the forces of evil".

He said standing up straighter holding his weapon a modified sawn off shotgun, it shiny with writing all over it,

"Meet me here at the same time tomorrow, it seems we have a common enemy, and we could help each other".

The dweller said, the man nodded and quickly left, he did not follow but could of easily done he wanted to do it properly not scare them away, they seemed the God fearing types but it did not matter, he was not alone in his battle they would need an army, he moved back to his tower it felt good to be part of something and not so alone, if they would except him among them then they might stand a chance he thought.

3

Lucy Laurence entered the growing city of York having heard great things about it and the quick growth of its industries, an almost rise overnight. She had travelled from America, not an easy trip. But was curious as were her people, well her employer, they needed to know who the Fair Ones really were and Lucy was the best at her job, if there was a story here then she would find it and the deeper and darker the better, the more sordid it was the more it would sell.

Lucy was tried after her long trip and was already pre booked into a hotel just down from the train station her expenses were covered too. A meeting was already set up for her that evening and to actually meet an elder of the Fair Ones too, she was excited to say the least. She took a nap, bathed and dressed nicely then took in the amazing sights and sounds; the Minister being one of them then it was time to meet the new strange people with their unusual pointed ears, handsome, beautiful and well-spoken with manners. The restaurant was expensive and he had already arrived and gave her a little bow he was tall with red hair with yellow and orange eyes, his clothes were a suite of fine materials it sparkled with golden trims.

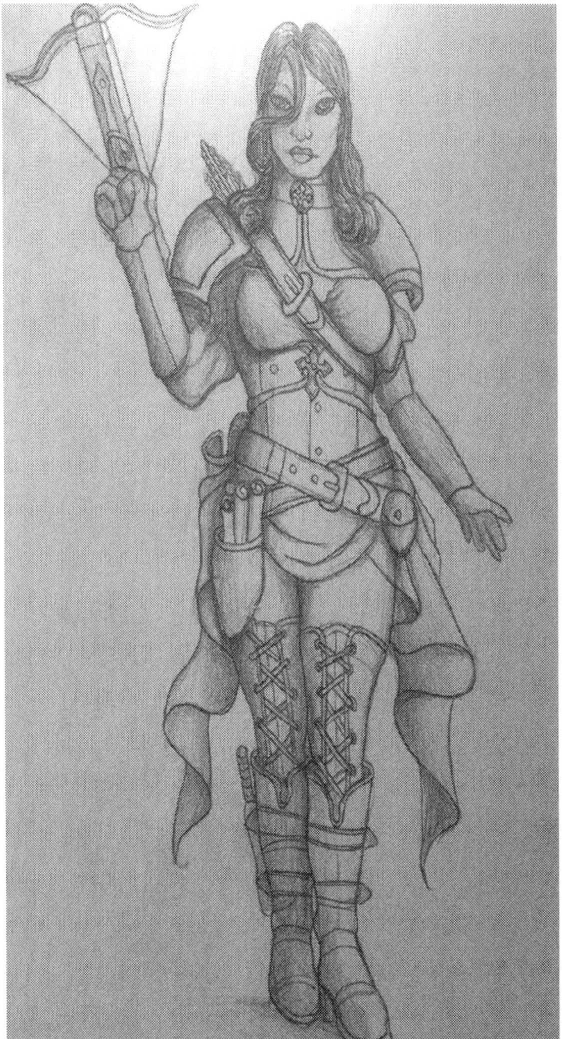

"My name is Rathan Stone, I heard that you are American, we have yet to visit your fine land, which I'm sure will change".

He said and was a very charming fellow, they were seated and food brought very quickly, he ate a salad with fruits and nuts, no meat, while Lucy had steak.

"So what brought you here and why choose York".

She started off her questions.

"We have brought much, science, metallurgy, the constellations, Astrology how to develop to gain knowledge become more than you are".

"What's the catch here, there's always a price".

She said and he just smiled Lucy was not sure if she liked the expression on his face.

"You have everything to gain from us and only want to share our vast knowledge".

"Many people have lost work, you have done more harm than good, there are poorer, and what will you do to address these problems".

"There will always be others that resent what we have done, what you speak of is over exaggerated".

He said then ate, Lucy had a keen mind for details and a great reporter, knowing how people spoke and reading between the lines and she was starting to see this Fair One was lying and avoiding and dodging her questions, he was like a politician, she was determined to get more out of him.

"So where do you come from originally and do you like being called Fair Ones".

"We come from a far land beyond yours, as for the name we do have a natural beauty and strength".

"You spoke earlier about America, do you wish to move further afield".

"In time yes, we have so much to give".

"How do you all know so much, and the technology you have brought with you where did it come from".

"It was handed down to us from those that came before and our ancestors".

Rathan Stone said, Lucy could see he was getting antsy and decided to close the interview knowing she was not going to get much more out of him.

"Well thank you for your time and opportunity to speak with you tonight". She said and went in to shake his hand which he took in his smooth cool hands and gently kissed the back of her hand and gave her that predatory smile and flash of perfect White teeth that looked very sharp, he made her shudder but not in a good way and she was glad to be out of his company and headed back to her room but could not shift her feeling of uneasy and the interview had not given her much to go on, her next task was to interview the workers and the families, people on the streets and other Fair Ones. She was feeling drained, tired and so took to her bed.

The next day Lucy took to the streets and shops first, asking general questions about what they thought of the Fair Ones, many were mixed some liked them and what they had done and brought, others hated them saying they were taking over and devouring their works and even people had gone missing some found dead, this intrigued her and she was starting to see a different picture forming and not a fair one either she thought and smiled to herself, thinking it would make a great future head line. Her next destination was the poor houses and it surprised her to find not so Fair Ones there too, many were mixed in and looked just as ill, sore and overworked, covered in soot and oil, and witnessed right away there was an hierarchy among the Fair Ones, much like their own working class and the rich they did not interact with those thought lower than them, then another surprise there was one of the higher ones working there, Lucy approached this new one, she was very pretty, red hair piercing yellow and orange eyes, and of course tall and sleek, Lucy was not tall she had wide hips and black hair and attractive in her own way and a total contrast to this Fair One. She smiled and seemed a lot more approachable.

"My name is Lucy, I'm a reporter from America, I'm doing a story about the Fair Ones, could you answer some questions please".

Lucy said it as politely as possible she was used to pushing her way in bold as brass, having learned quickly in the reporting industry, that it was not a place for women but she was no push over and wanted to change that.

"That depends on how you portray us".
She said.

"My eyes have been opened, I've seen the top and now the lowest part and see you getting your hands dirty, I will make it as honest as possible".
Lucy said.

"Honesty is the best policy, I don't work here because of pity or guilt for having more than these people. I don't care for their decadence, showing what we brought in a positive light is great and all, we are not proud of our past, I will do my part".

"Do you see things getting any better here,or at this level, the parts nobody sees, we see the steam machines and the massive factors, and the smog".

"No, there will be a reckoning and things will get worse before they get better, there is a lot more going on here than meets the eye, the deeper you dig the more you will find but you might not like it".

"I'm a reporter digging is what I do best, do you and your people want to be laid bare like that, because all your dirty linen will be on show".

"Then do what you must, I have nothing to hide".

"What can you tell me about the deaths and disappearances that have grown in number since your people's arrival".

"A dark cloud has always hung over us, we only show what we want you to see".

"I've heard that before, it's call the government".

Lucy added.

"There have been a number of fatalities, which we have been investigated".

"Thank you for your time, I think your people should be more like you".

Lucy said and the Fair One handed her a business card with a cog on it for a brief moment they touched hands which gave her a tiny shock and went back to her duty, Lucy felt dizzy she saw mountains and wide valleys and a bright light and flames and was transported back to her youth, she did not remember returning to the room, she felt warm and had to sit down, she saw her father and the work that had driven her family apart, he had been a Reverend they were a very religious family but what he found was self-consuming, he would spend hours in his study, they would barely see him. He said he had found the book of Enoch and translated this ancient Jewish religious work and she knew this secret document back to front, a lot of the wording was hard and full of parables, metaphors and it was not liked by the church and deemed non canonical. She had helped her father and it was good for a time, spending time with him, even going to university to study ancient languages such as Aramaic and of course Latin. Then it hit her, the documents similarities to what she had just learned, there were key words that stood out, such as *to devour the works of man then went onto kill man.* Metallurgy, weaponry and fine jewellery that adorned their fine clothes. It was what they were doing and it was happening right then. the Fair Ones were the offspring of Angels and man, they were Nephilim or Giants which did not have to mean they were massive tall beasts she hoped, and if it was happening again then danger was coming with it, Lucy know this was bad what they had brought with them, Lucy hoped it was coincidental but who would believe her and who could she go to with this knowing how crazy it sounded to her, she was a religious woman having read the bible too, it had been her upbringing but the signs were there a feeling deep in her gut and that touch with the female helper the images that were right out of that book. Lucy paced the room wishing her father was there, he would have known what to say and do, she decided to seek help from the church and visit the Minster tomorrow, Lucy slumped onto the bed and slept like the dead, her dreams full of religious images and metaphors.

*

Adam Watts did his usual shift but was not about to leave what he had seen alone, walking his beat he would ask people who might of witnessed attacks or deaths but they seemed too afraid to come forwards, some spoke of an urban legend. The Dweller, who took the young from their beds, always watching. But others said the

Dweller was not evil and even helped people, but this did not fit the death he had seen and was not from a legend who took people away this was very different, and so he had hit another dead end no pun intended he thought and wanted to meet this dweller. He too might have been a witness or know something and his own force was no good even the J.O.T.P(Justice of the peace) turned a blind eye to it, even threatening him to leave it alone, there had been more with the same but he could not get anyway near the case not like that was about to stop him, so instead of asking about the deaths it was the Dweller he wanted to question and they seemed more willing to talk about that a mysterious figure then a real threat but at least it was something to go on, so he went to places around the city where there had been sightings and witnesses he mapped them out in his head hoping to narrow his investigation to pinpoint where he might be working from or living, then Adam looked up seeing marks on the walls this Dweller was using the rooftops to move, witnesses would report him being at one part of the city then appearing somewhere else so could move fast up there.

There had been a disturbance and shots fired he went to the scene in an alleyway that lead down to the river in the city centre just off Coney Street it had been raining a lot lately so the water was higher than normal it was muddy and so there were two sets of boot prints one very heavy the other a lot smaller but there was something else odd there was a set of bare feet but they did not look human or Fair Ones who had small feet the big toe was large with a gap between them and looked deep but that was all he managed to see the rest had boot prints from other constables and the public he just wish he could of closed the scene off somehow and even the smallest details were important and could be used as evidence but when he even suggested such a thing they would just look at him as if he was crazy or just laugh. He told them that one day it would happen and be a science, he used his keen eyesight and quick mind and work with what he had so there was substance to the stories there was always a truth and he was going to get to the bottom of it.

Adam Watts wanted to speak with the Fair Ones and not the working ones there were two types one the leaders they were tall and thinner acted like royalty looked down on all that were not them and they did not mix with humans that much and even had their own part of the city, then there were the workers these were smaller with stocky build, strong and tough. They would work alongside the humans and were more approachable, it still caused friction his people resented them, saying they were stealing their jobs even though they brought more work with their arrival, the big factories employed both and equally.

But there was one and she helped the poor and not just her own kind but humans too and if she knew anything else about the deaths or the Dweller, with her been so close to the poor and needy that would not speak to the law and she would know how to ask those higher, he would need sleep first though so he finished his shift for the night and headed back to his small apartment and dropped on to the bed tried, feet hurting, it was a lonely life working the night shift with nobody to come home to, it was hard he put a little of his wage aside in the hopes of finding a woman but right now it was the force he was married too and she was hard especially with them turning a blind eye, it was not the job he was expecting he knew it was hard work and he was making little or no difference at all, it was very frustrating he was never going to make a dent if every time he took a step forward they would send him back two it was like they did not want him pocking his nose into things they seemed so corrupt either wanting a quiet life and not wanting to rock any boats so Adam Watts was going to take things into his own hands but right then he needed sleep.

Adam Watts hardly had any days off with the force been so stretched so he had to wake early and head into the City's centre the Fair Ones used the Mayor's office but they would turn him away the trouble was he did not know the name so he headed for the homeless shelters and refused and it would have to be potluck and trying to avoid other constables which made him feel guilty even though he was not doing anything wrong, he was dressed in civilian clothes, the first shelter he came to was very busy he felt bad and stuck out like a sore thumb it smelt bad and saddened him too, there was just no help for them, the church helped where they could but they had been losing their numbers of late due to the industrialisation and urbanization were to blame for the decline and people were less god fearing and a lot more open minded about things such as science, becoming more curious, he too felt this way it was becoming a new age where many were stuck in their ways of the past and how things were done and so there was resentment animosity. But times were changing and he wanted to move along with it.

There were no Fair Ones there so he moved onto the next place, this time he asked one of the human helpers and described who he was looking for, the thin man nodded and pointed to the Fair
One and smiled, he saw her pointy ears first she stood tall with fine red hair and she was the typical type elegant and pretty but she was different she had a smudge of soot on her high cheek bone and instead of fine clothes she wore plain trousers a blouse and a stained apron around her thin waist, sleeves rolled up it was then he felt himself staring at her in an admiringly way. Adam

watts approached the Fair One Female, she gave him a warm smile and moved a piece of hair from her face and tucked it behind the long pointed ear which had ear rings.
"Can I help you sir".
She said in a light smooth voice they were an enchanting race and many a man had lost their hearts to these fair people indeed, his mind went blank for a moment then he managed to speak.
"I'm a constable Adam Watts and have been trying to investigate these disappearances of late and have been interested in a fellow called the dweller".
His statement seemed to put her off guard for a moment.
"I'm Ithilli Norium What do you wish to know, I'm sure he has nothing to do with the murders".
She said.
"Well your right it doesn't fit, but he could be an important witness, there is a lot of fear on the streets and I'm getting nowhere fast".

He said.

"You're not like the other constables or humans for that matter".

She said.

"So others have questioned you on this and the Dweller?"

He said. And she nodded and took him off to one side.

"My own people are going missing too, you seem very caring, so let me warn you to leave this case alone no good will come of this investigation".

She said in a quiet voice and seemed nervous looking around.

"Well I've already been told to leave it and threatened too".

He said.

"You are a strange one, and I like that but believing what I'm going to tell you is another thing".

"I'm quite open minded, and after seeing the looks on the corpses face. Like they had been scared to death".

"We can't talk here about this, meet me after dark on Parliament Street, there is much talk about".

She said and he agreed to it, he returned to his apartment and tried to get some more sleep but all he kept thinking about how her yellow and orange eyes that seemed to sparkle with a wildness and animalistic, then he left in a daze but his mind soon cleared, it was busy now but he still felt guilty going behind his own people, something was going on and more than just murders and disappearances, there were cover ups, he wondered what internal affairs might think, he did not want them involved though, they were his friends and colleagues but even this was testing his loyalty.

Adam Watts started his shift the same as usual and did not rush straight there not wanting to seem so keen and to make sure he was not been followed it was a quiet night and the smog hung low in the narrow streets as if sticking to everything it touched, he saw her in a long black hooded cloak. He quietly approached her but she turned as if knowing straight away he was there.

"Come with me now, and bring with you your open mind".

She simply said then started walking he followed and had to keep pace with her.

"There is evil Mr Watts, things beyond of what a human can grasp and see, and we are all been stalked by it. But there are those among us that are outside these rules and your own people too who see through the Vale, I believe the dweller is one of them".

It mostly went over his head it did not help that they spoke so poetic and cryptic all the time.

"I hope you are ready to step into this world, I believe he is connected in some way to this as are you now".

She said as they approached the river.

"We are an ancient race Adam and our lives are long, we came to you with our knowledge only wanting to help, but with good comes the bad, we all have a history and ours goes way back".
"So who is behind the murders".
Adam Watts asked.
"It would be our past, but my people have turned a blind eye to it living in denial, the corruption is among us all now, be mindful of this, they may already be in places of power and influence".
She said.
"But how do we know who they are, I hope you know how crazy all this sounds".
"Yes and I am sorry, there is no other way but to just tell you and I will even show you, but not now, I've already said too much, don't speak of this, I will be in contact with you soon Mr Watts".
He was about to ask her when but she and gone, it was a lot to take in he went back to his beat trying to get his head around what he had just stumbled into.

*

A knock at the door made Sarah Newcomen jump, her pulse quickened, most of the time it was letters or some other things, the maid or servants would deal with, the knock came again there was no Mary which meant she would have to answer it and was about to ignore it when she saw that it was one of the Fair Ones and not just some worker but one of the high ones and was not the demons, she hesitated then slowly opened the door a little and peered out she was tall and slim the usual look for them and very pretty.
"Lady Newcomen, I'm Ithilli Norium I am a liaison representative of the Fair Ones, I believe you requested a meeting".
She said in a smooth light voice, it had been a very quick reply and had taken her by surprise, which made her suspicious but seen as she was here Sarah Newcomen let her in then looked up and down the garden and locked the door once more and lead

the Fair One into the lounge, there was an awkward silence as Sarah Newcomen tried to find a way to put it into words and try not to sound crazy at the same time or just blurt it out, she remembered this one most of her kind hated the humans but this one had some sympathy and might be the one she needed.

"I knew my people took a long time to except you and trust you even longer. And have done a lot for us and there is no way I would threaten this".

Sarah Newcomen paused for a moment trying to gauge the Fair One.

"I've seen through your vale of illusion, those that are good among you have a healthy glow about you but I have also seen something darker among you and my people, an evil is growing".

Sarah had not spoken of this to anybody for years and it felt great too, she looked at the Fair One again waiting for her to rush out and call the lunatic wagon and drag her away again, but she just slowly nodded then with a faint smile on her lips she spoke.

"I'm happy you came to me and must have taken courage to tell me, they hide from us too and we can sense them around us. What you have is a gift".

"I would not call it that, people think I'm crazy and should be locked up, it's a curse but a least it is real and not just in my mind, you get called crazy for so long you start to believe them".

Sarah said.

"You are not crazy, we are guilty of hiding our true selves from you for those simple minded it would be scary for them to accept us for what we are, we have never had any ill intentions and have given freely what we know".

Ilthilli Norium said.

"What will you do with what you have learned, what can I do to make them stop".

Sarah Newcomen said.

"Firstly tell nobody, if they are up wind of you, then you may be in danger, secondly there is another who has witnessed the evil you have seen, we must all fight this together".

The fair One said, Sarah had never felt so relieved it was like a weight had just been lifted, wishing she had done this sooner and for another to have seen the same has her too lifted her heart.

"So where to now, how can I use this".
Sarah Newcomen said.

"I can get you in touch with him, but he has used science to see what you see naturally, he is called the Father and he fights the evil that is unseen and denied by my own people".

Ilthilli Norium said then gave her a business card it had a simple design of a cog on one side and an address on the other.

"Stay strong Sarah and be careful, we will speak again".

With that she left and Mary returned and looked confused at seeing her lady smiling, she flipped the card in her fingers this meant she would have to leave the house and face her fears.

"Is everything ok my lady, is there anything you need".

Mary said having not seen the visitor.

"I couldn't be happier Mary, get me ready I'm going out".

Her servant almost dropped her shopping and gasped.

"Right away my lady".

She said and hurried off.

*

Lucy Laurence took in the sights and sounds of the growing city, ate out and shopped it was not an all business trip, but every time a Fair One walked passed her it was at the back of her mind, what she had seen and learned made her look at them differently like they had something to hide, she became a little paranoid too, did they know what I know she thought. Lucy headed down Stonegate and saw the Minster through the buildings it was truly massive to her, she entered feeling the cool air to find the place deserted, it was just as impressive on the inside and made her stomach feel funny when looking up in the main high towers, walking passed the pews and chairs, the statues and stained glass winds it was then that she was approached by a priest or a vicar as she had learned they were called in England.

"Can I help you young lady, we don't get many people in here since the so called Fair Ones arrived".

He said the man was of average height, thinning grey hair, softly spoken and lined faced which reminded her of her father.

"As it happens it's them I need to speak about, I'm an investigative journalist and have been doing a bit of digging around and asking questions, they are not loved by all and seemed to have a few secrets too".

Lucy said but was not sure how to even brooch the subject, thinking they would cart her off for being crazy she thought, so

feeling a little nervous and embarrassed decided to just come out with it, but needed to word it carefully.
"I believe the Fair Ones to be the Nephilim, and their intentions are to take over and devour us all".
"And how have you come to this conclusion".
He said but looked very serious.
"In a vision father, the signs are all around us, I of course hope I'm wrong, and I know how crazy this sounds".
"How did you come by this conclusion, and how would you know about such religious things".
He sounded condescending as if a woman should not know such things, Lucy felt and was starting to regret her decision coming here.
"Come we could discuss this further in my office".
His face had changed and did not look so kind anymore, his once gentle eyes now looked wicked.

"Maybe i shouldn't have come".
she said backing away from him.
"You came to the right place child, we can't ignore the signs and visions, what is your name".
he asked and made a grab for her arm but she was too fast and ran out of the Minster right into a boy all but knocking him over she said sorry and rushed back to her room to find it all in a mess, her clothes on the floor her paperwork too, but they had not found anything it was all in her note book which she kept on her person but still had to check if it was there, on looking she found another business card which must have been from the boy she thought when they had collided, it was the same one the Fair One had given her with the cog on it, there was a date and time to meet at the homeless shelter where they had first met. she had to sit down feeling light headed, it was hot too and a lot to take in Lucy was beginning to wonder what she had just stumbled into, she turned the card over in

her hand then remembered her father's paranoia he told her to watch her back and that people wanted his work and that they were always watching and that they too had a break in, and now this. Lucy was not afraid in fact it put her investigative mind into overdrive. In her younger days she had met a young man called Matthew King, well fell for him. but in the end he had only just being using her to get to her father, and was part of some religious zealots that called themselves the Elect, well a twisted version and self-appointed, they scared her though and she did not want to know what they were capable of or have done, they were there in York all the way from America, they had followed and did indeed seem to be everywhere. she cleaned up the room not wanting to bring in the Justice of the Peace, the Elect were most likely in there too. Lucy was determined to not let their scare tactics get the better of her. She packed up and quickly left to find another place to live she was not going home just yet, now more than ever she wanted to get to the bottom of this, she found a bed and breakfast on Stonebow it was called the Golden Fleece and was supposed to be haunted which did not bother her having far more scary things after her. They had a room which was nice enough a little small for her taste but clean, it was just a base now and place to work from. That meeting on the card was not until later she tried to get some rest but her nerves were in tatters but did manage a little nap.

Lucy left the Golden Fleece and headed over to the shelter it was getting late and the streets were nearly empty which made it easier to spot anybody following her, she kept looking behind nervously as she reached the place and there was the tall elegant Fair One tidying up as the last few left for the night, the place was a soup kitchen, she saw Lucy and waved her over.

"I'm sorry for the delivery serves for my card, you are in danger which I'm sure you are already familiar with".
She said in a kind smooth voice.
"You saw it too didn't you, the vision when we touched of which I'm sure was no accident".
Lucy said and the Fair One smiled.
"There are others like you that have become known to them as have you, come and meet them and your eyes will see everything, please trust me they are closing in on you".
"This all sounds good but i have my own problems too and they are called the Elect, they have always been after my family and are here in York".
"I'm already aware of them too, it's all connected, and the address is on the card".
Lucy looked down and flipped it over and was sure there was no other writing on it, but it was there. She looked back up but the Fair One had vanished. Lucy returned to the Inn rushed inside and locked the door to

her room and sat on the bed wondering what had just happened, having come to find out about the mystery of the Fair Ones and was finding out a lot more than she had bargained for and felt like she was sinking under it all, she played with the card between her fingers flipping it over then looked at the address again knowing she needed help.

*

Adam Watts arrived at work, the Sergeant glared at him he could not understand why the man did not like him. He changed and put on his uniform ready for his shift and found a business card tucked in the pocket with a picture of a cog on one side and an address on the other and a name written on it, Ilthilli. He smiled on seeing the Fair Ones name it was worth checking out but he would have to be careful he was already doing more than he should and his questioning would not go unnoticed but he would just deny it anyway, so he started to do lot of his shift first and be seen doing his beat, the address was on the outskirts in the industrial district a bit out of his way but he was curious why she was sending him there.

It was getting late but it was still very busy the factories pumping out their smoke never stopping or sleeping, the card brought him to a small workshop the lamps were on when he knocked at the door and was greeted by a female Fair One worker she was short and heavy set large breasts, wearing dirty overalls and a heavy leather welders apron and white circles around her eyes where the goggles had been, she looked worried on seeing a constable at the door which was most people's reaction, Adam showed her the business card and the name, the female nodded went back inside for a long moment then came back and let him in, it was dark and hot inside and smelt of metal and oil which seemed to be coating everything, tools hung on the walls with cogs and other mechanical devices he did not know what most did or what they were for, having worked with his father when he was a young lad, he was lead further in, it opened out into a large area and right in the middle stood a very

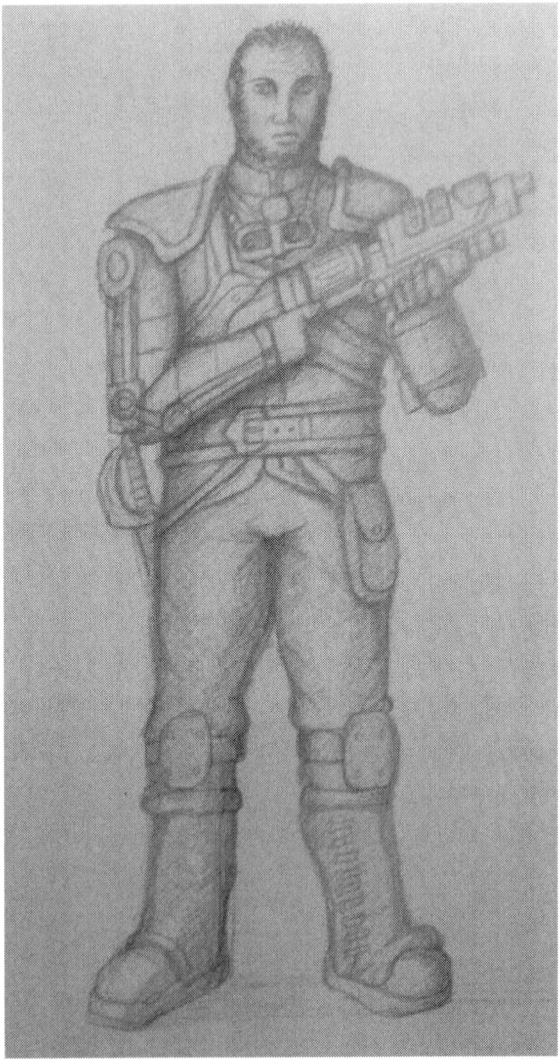

strange half Strangely built steam engine/train with more tools and parts which he had to step over it did not look very organised or safe for that matter, he was left at what looked like an office door, Adam knocked and entered, it was a small poky room with drawings and bits of paper and a cluttered drawing board and untidy desk the man in the room who face him now was very stocky fellow with glasses on his nose which had other lenses that looked like they could be slotted in and out with a brown tint, he had a round face and double chin with unkempt sideburns with brown hair, looked at his pocket watch, it was big with intricate parts and tiny dials and hands, then looked at the new comer.
"So you must be another Ithilli recruit. Welcome my friend, call me George".
The man said in a very broad northern accent, with a good nature and a sparkle in his blue eyes he wiped and offered his hand and give him a firm handshake, Adam was confused by what was supposed happening

and why he was meeting this man, the man looked around his untidy desk lifting thing up as he seemed to be looking for something while mumbling to himself then made an ah noise then handed him a small monocle made of tan coloured glass.

"There you go lad, you wish to see what is going on, then come with me but once you have seen there's no going back".

He said then big man lead him through a wall panel off the small office which turned into a door, the passage beyond was rough brick that lead them from his building to the one next door, it was a very busy and noisy textile workshop with huge weave machines that were steam powered there was a fair one working on it.

"Right then see him yonder the fair un, now look at him through the lens I gave you".

He said Adam did as he was told, again confused at it all so he looked through it at the male Fair One and what was once tall and handsome now was a twisted evil version with long bony arms long neck half of which was wrinkles and a massive mouth full of horrid rotting teeth, then he took the lens away and almost dropped it, the big man grabbed Adam and pulled him away so as not to alert it, and took him back to the workshop were Adam was still in shock and looked pale he cleared a space for him to sit for a moment.

"They hide among us, and even looking like us to, I designed it so we can see what we are fighting, they are in our government and police, spreading their poison and corruption, now not all Fair un's are like this so we have to be careful how we go about this".

George said.

"So who can we tell or report this to, I don't understand how this is possible".

Adam said.

"Well we can't tell just anybody or every one, remember what the Fair un's have brought, the tech and knowledge would be lost it would destroy the economy in a matter of weeks".

"So you fight these things in secret, so these are responsible for the murders and the missing".

"Yes and yes, and they are not easy to kill either, so this is where I come in, will you join our fight?"

Now Adam could see why he was there and that his persistence and investigation had paid off, he had cracked the case but could not do anything with it or tell anybody, it was frustrating with this dark world hidden beside their own, unseen he could see why they were stuck and how careful they must act and what would happen and look like if they were caught be the Justice of the peace that were already corrupt, this made him wish he had not known now ignorance was bliss he thought, and was afraid of what he saw but wanted to fight this all the more.

"Sign me up George".

"Well done lad, that's the spirit".

George said and slapped Adam on the back nearly knocking him over and left him slightly winded.

"There will be a meeting soon you will be contacted where and when we are not sure if those bastards know of us yet but we have to be careful".

George added. The female worker knocked and entered she stood with George.

"Don't speak of this, go about you usual routine, use the lenses carefully and discreetly only observe who the Evil Ones are and where they are, we know it is a shock at first, and they have been on the increase too".

She said.

"This is Jillith you can trust her, she helps me with my work".

He said.

"He means crazy inventions".

She said the two acted as if they were together as a couple and it was not unheard of For Fair Ones to be with humans. Adam Watts said goodbye and had spent far too long away from his beat and get back to his work there was no need to investigate now that he knew that monsters were responsible in both the literal and physical sense, he kept seeing it in his mind it had disturbed him he felt the lens in his pocket turning it over, wanting to use it on everybody and remembered what the female Worker One had said but it did not stop him feeling paranoid flinching at moving shadows out the corner of his eye until his shift finally ended it was not until he was back in his apartment did he feel he could relax a little bit, he did not sleep too well his dreams were full of monster and creatures which did not leave his thoughts even while awake the big man had been right, there was no going back.

Adam Watts walked in to work and was meet by the sergeant with his big moustache and round belly and a bad attitude, he called him in to the office and told him he was fired and to collect his things.

"What have I done, you can't just sack me like this".

Adam Watts said demanding.

"You were warned about pursuing the murders, you are just a constable that needs to do as he is told, and if you are caught anywhere near this again you will be seeing our cells from the wrong side".

The sergeant said with a smug look on his face.

"You have not heard the last of me or this I will take it higher do you hear me".

Adam Watts said wishing he could tell this man what was really going on and what was behind it all, and that they did not want him nosing around and finding out how corrupt they were it was frustrating not been able to say anything when all he wanted to do was rub the man's face in it and kick his fat arse out of there and sack him not that he did any work he imagined.

"Do what you will but if you raise your voice to me again then you will be in a cell". He said. Adam Watts had to walk away know it would do him no good in a cell while he know what was really going on and besides that he could now work with George and the Fair One female, so he left a little disappointed but there were things happen that were bigger than his ambition to be an officer of the Justice Of the Peace he would still be doing the work just not officially, he got back home and found another business card with the cog on the other side was a different address two letters G.S so with nothing else to do he had to go find a map and find that address it was on the outskirts of the City the newer part that he did not know like the city centre it was growing more and more every day it seemed, in the end he had to hire a carriage to take him there it was a single horse drawn and he gave the driver the address he just nodded and held the door open Adam Watts climbed in and took the bumpy ride across the city knowing his rent would be due soon having never been sacked before it was upsetting a blow to his ego even if it was not entirely his fault, but at that moment it was something he would have to deal with later because if things got any worse he might not have a home to go back to.

The ride took almost one hour to reach, it was further out than he thought it might be, he climbed out paid the driver the horse left behind a big pile of crap leaving him with a bad smell and another long walk it was a long driveway with trees on either side his boot crunched on the gravel he reached a big gate and walls either side it was open he stepped through then had another long walk but this time he was face with a huge house or hall it had a grand entrance with rose of windows and red brickwork but has he got closer he could see it had seen better days and was in need of some work it was quiet and he was starting to wonder if he was at the right place not thinking to of kept the driver but he was there now so he knocked but with no answer after knocking again but louder he walked round the back and found more out buildings a court yard and stables here he heard hammering metal on metal as he came round to it the building was a massive forge with anvils and tools the heat hit him as he entered, the forge was big with a chimney above it and big bellows used to keep the fire hot it was Jillith the short powerful woman was covered in black soot and carrying a massive hammer that even he would struggle to lift never

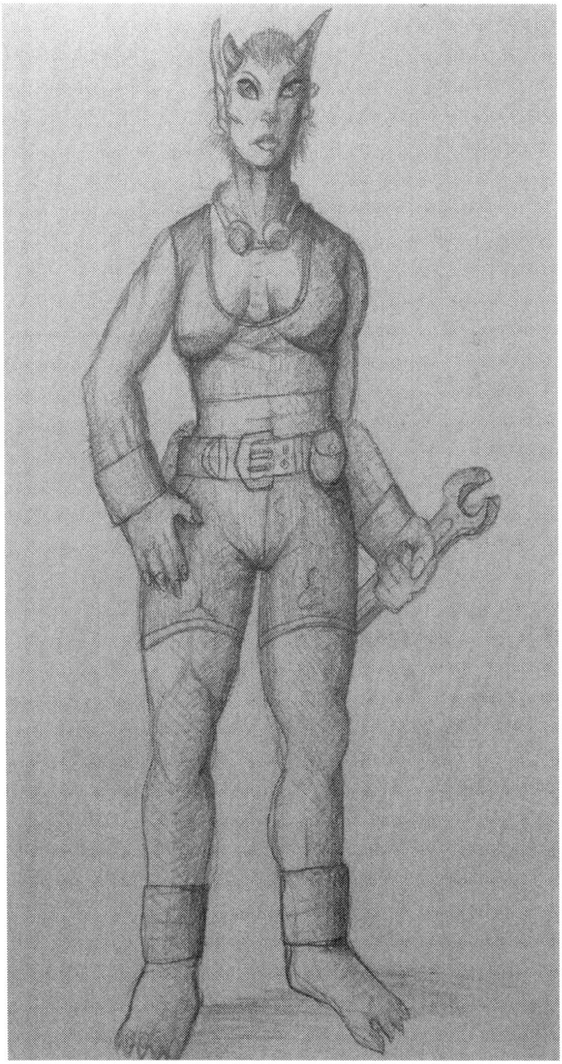

mind use like she seemed to be doing quite effortlessly she stopped on seeing him and he was glad because his ears were ringing.
"Your early, he's not back yet but I'll take you to the waiting area".
She said.
"Yeah sorry about that I was sacked today so I have nothing else to do now".
Adam Watts said.
"Well ok I trust you said nothing about this whole thing".
Jillith said.
"It was from before we met and I kept investigating the murders which they had warned me off doing, it was hard but I kept silent".
Adam Watts said.
"Yes we all have lies to keep up, and I'm sorry to hear that you were sacked but sacrifices have to be made for us to continue our work in secret".
She said has she took him inside the building it was surprisingly cool, compared to outside, the weather was changeable but

summer was coming in hard with relentless heat which his night shift usually took him away from, leaving him to wonder how all those workers did it in the factories that were already hot enough the decaying building did not look much better on the inside there were dead leaves and dust on what was once a tiled floor ivy grow on the inside.

"Don't go wandering around this place it is in need of a lot of work, especially upstairs the flooring is rotten in places, just wait here, there is no staff or maids all will be explained".

With that said she left him to his thoughts, he could not help a quick look but stayed on that floor there were chandeliers full of dust and cobwebs faded and dusty paintings on the walls too dark and cracked to see he returned to the reception area again and sat down on an old faded chair it creaked but held, it was not long before he became restless and tired having not slept yet and dozed off in the chair a door opening woke him it was Ithilli Norium she seemed to float across the floor it was a very seductive walk she looked stunning as ever, the summer sun shone from behind it seemed to form a glow around her or it was just his blurry eyes.

"I'm glad you answered our call, you were meant to be here, do you have the lens".

She said in her smooth voice he told her of his first meeting with George, what he had seen and him been sacked and ending up there.

"It has all happened for a reason Adam, this will be your new home don't worry about rent or food all will be provided here, so you have first chose on a room with less rot".

She said with a smile that made his pulse race but he controlled himself and his emotions knowing their Fair charm and influence.

"So who is George, and what are we going to be doing here".

Adam Watts asked needing to calm his loins so changed the subject he know she would have no interest in him that way it was unheard of for the high Ones to have an affair let alone talk to humans, and yet she was different in that respect.

"George is a man a head of his time a geniuses, he saw the evil beyond the Vale with science, and that's how we will defeat them we just need to learn of what they are planning and for that we need people who are unique like yourself to fight".

She said Adam did not consider himself unique or special his mind was finding it all very hard to take in and keep up, it was happening all at once it was hard to grasp that such evil existed there had always been stories of monsters and demons but that's all they had been then to actually see such things hurt his brain that and been afraid and there he was right in the middle of it all.

"I will let him explain his plan, I don't want to steal his thunder or ruin the surprise".

With that she left and Adam Watts went to go and find a room the wide curved stairs seemed solid enough which took him up to the second floor there were rose of rooms he carefully walked along the landing, looking into the rooms as he went some did not have a window or a floor some both others the doors just would not open then there was one that looked like somebody had recently been there many had keys so he took the room next to that, it was intact the wallpaper and plaster was in a bad way stained and rotten like everything in the place it had a window with faded curtains the bed was small and lumpy but would have to do, he wished he had brought his things, but not knowing this would happen he would have to that and leave his small apartment that he could not pay rent on any way or had that many possessions he did not want to leave on bad terms his father had helped him get his first place and would wonder where he had gone he was not going to tell him he was to become some demon hunter and who would believe him anyway he could hardly grasp it himself. He locked the door and left with what little money he had left he would need to hire a carriage but on telling Jillith this she got one of the other workers to use theirs the work that drove him to what would be his old home was a male he too was heavy set and full of muscles both sexes were like this and very strong this one did not speak and only grunted yes or no answers so Adam gave up and enjoyed the ride with no clues to has what was about to happen one thing he did know and that it was going to be one crazy and scary ride.

When the knock came to his door Edward Ludlam almost jumped out of his skin and after expecting to be sacked for breaking that weaving machine and besides it was not working very well in the first place so they had let him off to cool down for the rest of the day not knowing if he had a job to go back to but a young lad handed him a summons from the Fair Ones no less he was very confused that and a waiting carriage to take him he climbed in the single horse drawn and not just some taxi either it was very comfortable with a padded seat and not just wooden planks which made for a smooth ride he was still feeling apprehensive though it was not very often they spoke to humans let alone summon them the note just read.

Dear Edward Ludlam.

You are invited to attend a meeting with one of the high Fair Ones who wishes to speak with you concerning an urgent matter with regards to your further employment.

Yours sincerely
Rathan Stone

Edward Ludlam folded it back up, it was not long when they had arrived at the Fair One's headquarters they had taken over many of the royal houses to which they seemed at home in and accustomed to, he had to work long hours and shift work to make ends meet he shared a room with his workmates the conditions were appalling to say the least so when he was lead inside

this place the first thing that hit him was the smell or lack of, no sweaty bodies here it was very nicely decorated white high ceilings and chandlers, big mirrors he looked at himself now feeling very dirty and under dressed for this he was taken up stairs to a huge office bigger than his whole sleeping quarters with white walls and doors the Fair One stood looking very tall towering over Edward Ludlam he was handsome with bright piercing yellow eyes, high cheek bones red hair and the trade mark of the Fair Ones the pointed ears and red hair his clothe finely tailored and smart looking like royalty with their usual arrogant attitude this one looked down at him with pity he did not know which was worse.
"So why am I here, I'll pay for what I did". Edward ludlam said. But the Fair One smiled but there was no humour there, it looked wicked.
"No my dear human you won't be needed there any more, we have much to discuss".

He said in a smooth voice but it was more like a hunter speaking to its pray and he did not like this one bit.

"You have a choice, one you go back to that hot dirty factory or you work under me, you are to champion the workers' rights to give back what mass production has taken, for those who have lost work or been taken over".

He said then let it settle in but Edward ludlam was confused these people had brought this why was he doing this he felt there was no choice here but it did sound better than the factory and he would like to see the looks on their faces.

"Very well I'll work for you, does this mean my pay goes up and I can live somewhere else to".

Edward Ludlam said pushing his luck which he often did with people and women too and for the most part his cockiness paid off. The Fair One smiled again this time there was a small hint of humour.

"You are going to live better and smell better too we will talk again my assistant will show you out and where your accommodations will be, all will be explained and you won't be disappointed". With that said the tall Fair One just turned round leaving Edward stood there in an awkward silence and more confused than when he arrived, he left the office to be met by the young lad again who took him back to the carriage and would not answer any questions he acted a little strange too, the place he was taken was a lot bigger than he was used to in fact he had a whole town house to himself for now, thing were looking up for the good he thought and the first thing he did was get a bath and with running water and hot and cold no less there were clean cloths too. He wish he had broken that damn weaving machine earlier he thought with a smile, he soaked in the tubes hot water not wanting to get out, his parents had worked hard, long hours on the farm all year round trying to make a living the industrial revolution was supposed to make things easier but it had done the opposite it put small business and farms out of business they could not keep up with the big company's so he had to work in the factories and his mother and father but they were too old they had to sell everything and live in small over crowded homes and no better off now having to breath in the bad air with the smog and smoke with no more fresh air to breath they were pale and tried this was the same story everywhere and only the rich got richer, yes it had worked wonders for the country's economy but at what cost.

*

Peter Aldwark was a businessman and when the Fair Ones came it was a godsend and businesses boomed almost overnight and he had taken full advantage of this, he ruthlessly took over small businesses, then began exporting to Europe and even America, he became rich just as quick, he put Sheffield on the map they made steel and Scunthorpe too. The Fair Ones had brought so much, metallurgy, science, chemistry and of course steam they revolutionised everything, gave them the tools needed, brought structure and guidance how to run things, that's when one of the high Fair Ones came to him tall and smartly dressed Rathan Stone was his name, Aldwark knew it was a great honour to have them speak to humans but to come right to his office which made him very nervous indeed, it was a great thing and would be good look Amongst his peers and make them jealous too.

"I wish for your businesses to grow, the hard work you do has not gone unnoticed, we wish to spread further abroad and we want you to head this, to use your links". Rathan Stone said, Aldwark was very excited but acted calm and professional. "I will need full exclusivity, all will be running under and through me, and a full contract with my lawyers present. Before i let you have access to my contacts and clients".

Aldwark said and hoped he had not pushed him too hard, the Fair One smiled but it looked more like pure evil.

"Very well, it will be done. I knew we could count on you, you will be running it all for us, the company's and businesses will be yours, making you a very wealthy, a rich man with power and not just here in England but the whole world".

And with that said the Fair One just turned round and left, Aldwark could not contain himself for any longer, then danced around his office, he wanted it all, and was determined to get it having them all working under him, he could not wait to see their faces in the club later, they had laughed at his ambitions but not anymore, they would be working for him now. As he sat back down there was a letter addressed to him, his heart sank a little and know the writing right away, it was the Elect and right from the leader himself, it had been years since contact and he had all but forgotten about them, so to have received this all the way from America was not great timing for his business venture, the Elect hated the Fair Ones and anything new or different for that matter he thought, they were stuck way into the past. He was a sleeping member and when the call came one answered it, there would be others too, it was a simple note with just the leader's name, H.J. Longsfield. And that was it, Peter Aldwark sighed heavily it had put a dampener on his celebrations.

*

Lucy Laurence left the carriage and stepped onto the long gravel drive hoping she had made the right choice. The trees along each side of her were overgrown, it was mid-afternoon and the days heat was still in the air, then she saw the run down mansion, the front door was looked so she went around the back and was met by a Fair One worker, she was strong and stocky, Lucy told her that she had been told to come and showed her the business card once seen the worker smiled and told her to follow her inside, the air was cool and there was actually ivy growing on the inside of the building it looked like it might of been nice in its day, now there was peeling wallpaper and rotting plaster, faded and threadbare rugs and carpets. she was taken to a waiting room there was another girl waiting she was pale and dressed in back and looked worried and nervous just how Lucy felt and the pare sat in an awkward silence.

*

Adam Watts was settling in nicely there were set meal times more people were arriving it was very comfortable with a nice atmosphere he cleaned up his room and made it smell less fusty others helped with the house too putting in a few hours to help renovate the place or at least made it safer to walk around some had already put a foot through the rotten floor boards all had come from different walks of life all brought together either by George or the beautiful Ithilli and like him they did not have clue what was happening to them, then a meeting that evening was called and all had to attend maybe with some answers or bring more questions he thought. He left his room having been there three days now and a lot of the time it had been boring and he had to get his body clock accustomed to the day when he would have been normally asleep which made him feel tried that and not working was very odd but nice at the same time feeling like he was on holiday.

Then there was Richard a big man towering over everyone and even made George look small he was a wrestler and knew there host well he was a light hearted fellow laughing and making jokes mostly bad ones and tall tales. And called Adam Watts, Wattsy and made nicknames of everybody he could weather they liked it or not, he was down to earth but no way was he stupid but streetwise with a big heart any way he liked been around him he had a way to lift people's mood and with what they had all seen and witnessed it was great having him around.

Adam Watts found Richard in the overgrown grounds just walking about he saw him.
"Wattsy old boy what are you doing".
He said making Adam cringe at what he called him.
"I wonder what old George will have to say he likes new folk joining he's mind is always on the go coming up with some steam invention or some gadget".
Richard said swatting a fly with a big hand.
"Have you known him long".
Adam asked.
"Yeah we go way back we used to wrestle back in school, we both went different ways like you do then out of the blue he called

me up and showed me that lens of his and boy it changed my life, you never know what there is out there and what lies hidden".

He said but then he seemed to drift off into his thoughts for a moment.

"Come on Wattsy that Ithilli will be on her way and I know you will want a front row seat".

Richard said winding him up again as the two entered there was another man he was tall and strong looking but what stood out the most was the dog collar and a long black coat he was a preacher or vicar his face was weathered and looked like it had been chiselled out of granite.

"Preach not seen you in a while, must be important if you're here".

Richard said but he was just winding him up the Preacher sighed and shook his head.

"Might have known you would be here, but I guess we need all the help we can".

He said in a stern voice then was introduced to Adam, the man's hands were rough and

cold but a good strong hand shake there was nothing worse than a limp handshake.
"So you must be the Constable, god bless you in our fight".
"Don't start with that now Preach".
Richard interrupted him. A thin looking woman with black hair entered she was pretty wearing the fashion that most did but hers was a lot blacker more like something for a funeral, behind her was another woman she was a lot stockier and attractive too.
"Now that is lady Newcomen it is said she can see them without the lens".
Richard whispered to Adam, next came the Fair One Ithilli Richard elbowed him in the ribs which hurt, then George he was dressed very smartly and almost unrecognisable without the grease and muck his thinning hair combed back his voice boomed out in his broad accent.
"Thank you for coming and for joining us, we have a duty we can't let this evil go on and do nothing, but we have to be careful

you know of their far reaching corruption and they are everywhere".

He said with a way to hold a room all ears and eyes on him.

"So we are going to do the same we to will be everywhere watching them, and when the sun goes down they will not hunt us any longer we will hunt them".

They all liked what they heard; Jillith pulled in a trolley it looked heavy with a sheet over it.

"But to fight them we need and have a few tricks of our own".

A second trolley was wheeled in, he told them to step in closer as he pulled the sheet away he was been very dramatic there was what looked like a suit of armour looking like a knights of old but no quite as heavy and the helmet's visor was altered to have the glass lens and gas mask, then the next trolley was reviled in the same dramatic way but under this were weapons that were heavily modified a shotgun with a pump action that reloaded it, a pistol that could only be described as a hand cannon there were others too but all had been etched with swirly lettering the armour too, which he could not understand or even try to read.

"Now these are just proto types, a work in progress. The Dark Ones are strong and fast we are not, but each time we fight we learn more and become stronger, I won't lie it is dangerous and if caught by the law illegally, you will be put in prison".

He said and let them have a close look.

"I know you've all encountered the evil in one way or another or you would not be here, it is a very real threat and there is no telling what they are up to or what might be their end game, we won't go down without a fight".

With that said he handed over to Ithilli and wheeled the gear away.

"George is right even my own are under threat and have my backing there are others to who are willing to help and join you there are those who do like you among my people and are not hated as much as you think you are we need each other in this and we do need to put our differences aside, it's the only way".

She said Adam liked hearing her voice he had to concentrate which gave him a headache it would be good to see what she wanted but would never happen he thought knowing change would not come quickly.

"Rest now enjoy our hospitality, tomorrow the hard work starts".

She said and walked away the lady followed, food had been put out a buffet with nice posh nosh as Richard called it, Adam Watts ate far too much and went to bed early the shift work lag was still catching up with him.

*

It was a whole lot for Lucy to take in. She caught up with the tall Fair One who they called Ithilli. She had something important to tell her.

"Look can we speak in private; it's about what we spoke of earlier".

Lucy said and could not believe she had met the famous George Stephenson but it seemed he was leading a double life, even all the way in the states. He nodded to her and was not like what she had expected; Ithilli took her to one side.

"It's about the man you call Preacher, did you know he is a member of the Elect".

"We have known him for a long time now, are you sure".

"Yes because I was married to the man, he might not be who he says he is, come with me so I can confront him, he avoided me like the plague earlier".

"Very well lead on".

Preacher was eating and saw them coming over, Ithilli told him to follow them into the huge hall entrance and he looked worried to say the least.

"Matthew, I think this lady knows you, do you have anything to say to Lucy".

"You left me, and those Zealot friends of yours won't leave me or my family alone, have you lied to these good folk too".

Lucy said before he could even speak the two women stood arms folded waiting.

"They did send me here to York to keep an eye on George, but please believe me I left them after what he showed me, I only want to help".

Ithilli did not look happy.

"I will have to tell him, we trusted you, you're a vicar a man of God, and would you have told us".

Ithilli said and stormed off.

"Boy you have a way with women, have you truly left them, they are here in York, and have also followed me".

"I quit but one truly never leaves the Elect, there is a lot going on here, the Fair Ones are not quite who they seem, and for the Elect to get involved is bad, we have enough on our plates as it is".

"They must have also seen the connection with the book of Enoch and the Fair Ones, and they should see as you guys are mentioned in the damn thing".
Lucy said Just then Ithilli returned with George.
"I still need you, you are a valuable member of the team, for now you are excluded from meetings and plans until you can be trusted".
George said very disappointed with Preacher who just nodded looking down at his boots, when they left Lucy stayed to talk with him.
"You look terrible, do you eat over here in this rain in feasted place".
She said and did still care for the man, he did have a goodness deep down with good intentions but was also easily lead at times, the Elect leader was a smooth talker like an occult leader, working his way in, praying on the weak minded and knowing how to manipulate people and Matthew had fallen into that trap.

"Thanks, but you do look mighty fine though, it's not been easy escaping them and with what's going on here it has taken its toll on me".

"The Elect all but destroyed my family Matthew, my father is a shadow of his former self all because of that damn document, it's barely readable but they want it hidden away again, and will do anything to get their hands on it".

She said.

"If they are here we will have to contend with them and with the evil Fair Ones".

"All we can do is use your knowledge of them, what their next move might be".

"I will try to help and show I have put them behind me. I'm sorry Lucy for what happened between us".

"It's too little too late for that now, we are friends let's move on, and not tread old ground".

And with that said they parted ways, Lucy ate some food but it was getting late she found the Worker One so she could acquire a ride back to the city.

"You will be staying her now ma'am, your things will be brought here where it is safer for you, and training will begin".

"Wait a minute I'm not joining this little crusade of yours, I'm a journalist not a fighter, once I have my story I'm heading back state side".

The Worker One let out a sigh.

"Once you came here you're in, you can't go off telling everyone of this place and what we are doing here, it's a secret".

"Then I will publish it after all this is over, I'm not stupid, you think you have evil amongst your kind you haven't met the Elect".

At that point Ithilli came over to the two.

"its fine Jill, I'm heading back, she can come with me".

The Worker One quickly backed down and apologised, showing her how powerful the elite of the Fair Ones were. The two sat in the carriage as they were taken back to the city.

"Please don't fear the Elect Lucy, I won't allow it, I have contacts and will search them out for you".

"You don't need to do this, they are very powerful and influential, they have people everywhere they are called sleepers, and lay dormant sometimes for years until the call comes".

"I will bare this in mind, tell me more of this book of Enoch and it's similarities, we don't know that much about your one God, because we have many".

"You don't ask for much do you, I'll give you the basic principles for now, Enoch was of the seventh generation he was chosen to be shown what is beyond, he met the Lord of spirits and his angels, Enoch witnessed all of this and was supposed to have written it all down, but there are many interpretations and fakes my father and I translated it, there is a lot of controversy about what is written in there and so there are those who don't want it out".

Lucy said as the carriage bumped around. "It all sounds fantastic but what of the connection".

"Let's start with why our church doesn't like what it contains first, Angels are very powerful beings and their numbers are many and were supposed to have come down to Earth, our plane of existence and mated with humans their offspring were called the Nephilim and were Giants but they also brought with them forbidden knowledge such as weapons, metallurgy, agriculture and science. But these Nephilim grew restless and began taking over, consuming taking over the works of man and went on to kill and then eat them. Now such evil and fornication is frowned upon so the Lord of the spirits was not best pleased with such acts casting out the Angels and punishing them and upon the earth, a great flood was sent to cleans the world, now bare with me here this is a very simple

version I'm describing, I'm trying to break it down, so here comes the supposed connection, it's happening again and you are the Nephilim".
Lucy said then let it all sink in.
"Yes it almost fits, we have our own tales and myths, but one that stands out the most is the Ancient Ones, those that came before, they have many names such as the Watchers, but they were said to have been driven into the earth to be buried but they did make us, I supposed they could be mistaken for angels, there was once a massive battle between our people called The Blood Tide. And there are those amongst my people who would wish for a takeover, our world is dying we come from a different plane it is now corrupt and seeping into your world, so it is possible such a thing could happen here, so this lord of Spirits can he help again".
Lucy laughed.
"I'm sorry but it doesn't work like that here, were on our own".

"This one God of yours, he doesn't do anything what is the point in that, how very strange, so tell me more of this book and the Elect".

"There is yet more controversy, amongst the Parables and Metaphors, it mentions a rise of a Messiah a son of man, and this was 300 years BC, but it could mean the rise of another that and the Giants return. The Elect were also mentioned in the book but not the Zealots that are after us, they have interrupted it a lot different, twisting it to their own sick a gender and not affiliated with the church".

Lucy said, they had reached the city now. "Then it would seem we have much to prepare for, if there is anything else we should know, like how they will come".

"Speak with Matthew he was one of them, as for trusting him, i don't knew it has been years, it is difficult to leave a cult, when the time comes we will see how much hold there is over him".

And with that said she was dropped off at the Inn.

"We will speak again Lucy, watch your back".

Ithilli said and was gone, it was dark now and the air was fresh the Famous York Smog was settling in there was no telling what evil was out there. Lucy rushed inside and locked the door to her room which had not been turned over for once she though. Lucy was shaking when she sat down, she had not spoken of the book for years and it was bringing it all back for her, the trouble it caused was back to haunt her, thinking of her father so frail now. Lucy had always wanted to take the Elect down, they were always one step ahead but this time she had help and from the very ones they wanted to take down.

*

The young man he had rescued was there dressed in the armour, like they had arranged the Dweller dropped silently down making him jump and grip his weapon and the adrenaline rushed he smelt it making his own quicken.

"Come with me and I will take you to him". He said nervously the dweller nodded told him to lead on but he went back to the rooftops he could move quicker that way and could see and sense things before they were there, he jumped gaps with ease landing with a roll they were heading out of the city it was late in the hour as they came to a long drive with trees on the edge there were no building here to hide up or run across he felt vulnerable on the ground wondering where they were going the two approached the large Hall or Tang Hall as it was known he was taken to the rear what would have been the servant entrance the dweller knew there were more people here he could sense them smell and hear too, well above those that call themselves human but seem to possessed little humanity, so the man he now faced was a lot older and hard a large body that was slightly overweight he smelt of oil, dirt and worker female.

"Call me George, you are among friends, it seems you possess a strength we need to fight the evil stalking the streets, a common enemy".

The man said in a booming voice and accent.

"Yes but you seem ill equipped to fight them, I work alone you are too noisy and draw far too much attention with your clunky armour and those fire sticks".

The dweller said but he saw kindness in the big man even if he was in over his head in this, there was an innocence and goodness to him the dweller felt sorry for them but he had spirit and fight.

"Meet the others; join us if only for any advice or skills you have".

The man called George said, he agreed but did not know how he had just been talked into it, first a Fair One female and human female he knew they were there even before the door opened the one called Ithilli was familiar to him and the human female he could sense she had the Sight, and he could finally meet her face to face instead of watching from afar, she was different to the others and could see why they were been brought together here and such an undertaking might work with more of these special ones, they went down stairs the hall looked like it had seen better days his eyes saw well in the dark, any holes, weakness or dangers, here there were others a big one who was stronger than he realised a man of god and a man of the law the Fair Ones charm did not work on him, they all had potential he though gauging them.

"You are no mere myth then it seems, I was looking for you but have stumbled across a lot more".

The law man said the dweller saw him looking at the Fair One the humans pulse raced despite his immunity to the Fair charm, the seer human did not want to be there she did not like been surrounded by so many the strong one made jokes but there was a darkness within hidden by overcompensation he was very angry, lonely and sad but kept it inside, bottling it all up.

"So do you have a name".

The big one asked putting his hand out to be shaken, a human greeting he did not take it and shook his head.

"I don't know and have never needed one, I keep to myself".

"Then I will call you Smity, we can't go around calling you The Dweller all the time".

The one called Richard said he did not much like it or why there was a need for names or terms of affection, but for the sake of fitting in with them he nodded, the big man had names for the others too not that they liked it much either but he was very friendly and charismatic they were almost a family he just hoped the coming darkness would not break them, it was such a bond they would need he felt a pang a hint of emotion a longing to be a part of something an old feeling deep inside he had belonged to something before but the feeling was fleeting so on meeting them a he wanted to help, he looked at George who had a big smile on his face the Dweller knew he had just been had and gently manipulated there was a lot to this inventor and his crew of misfits. Maybe there was a chance but more of them would be needed and they would have to be stronger. He told them he would return and would keep his eyes open for any others who might have some ability or strength. He left them and returned to his rooftops with a feeling of hope well it was more of a glimmer but hope nonetheless.

*

Adam Watts awoke the next morning and could smell breakfast which was bacon mostly, he grabbed some food and a coffee, Richard had a massive plate full and a big mug of tea, Adam had more time to think about the one called the Dweller or Smity as Richard had given him he looked like the Fair Ones and the worker type strong and yet he looked tougher with similar traits as the evil ones with clawed hands no hair, high cheekbones a brow that looked like it was permanently frowning giving him an angry look quietly spoken with a wisdom beyond his years but another to the crazy line up of fighters he wanted to talk with him but the dweller had gone. George arrived with the new young lad, they ate and then he told them it was the start of their training and to wear the armour and weapons a fitting of sorts, once everyone had finished eating more trolleys were brought in with the armour and weaponry for four of them one had been modified for Richard with him been so much bigger he chose a massive Gatling type machine gun, or the G.M.G. as George called it they seemed suited, Adam Watts chose the hand cannon which was a revolver a new invention that held six bullets they were all given a rapier sword he had fired a pistol and was a good short but not the sword, next came the armour first he had to put on leather trousers and jacket then the armour was strapped on with the help of a worker it, was very heavy and cumbersome then the helmet was lowered onto his head it had round gas mask filters on either side the visor had round goggle lenses where the slits would have been he could not see out of it that well and it soon steamed up and became hot inside, he pulled it off and the other three were having the same problems George assured them the suits were a work in progress and would try to rectify anything to remedy it they remove the suits and they were taken away next they were instructed to bring their chosen weapon out to a makeshift firing range the ground of the Hall were big and overgrown targets had been set up with straw bales behind, the preacher had chosen a rifle he fired hitting dead centre the striped target was far off the young lad called Tom used a shotgun on a closer target then Richard turned his weapon on the target and tore it to shreds and the straw bale behind it they all held their ears and ducked for cover he laughed manically enjoying the destruction then it was Adam's turn his pistol was heavy and the recoil nearly tore it from his hand he hit the target just to the right of the bulls eye, for him it was close enough they all had a few more go's then went back to the Hall. They were shown a demo of sword play then fighting techniques with a little wrestling thrown in, then George wheeled in a tall chalkboard with a sketch of the evil ones.

"They are touch and fast and don't have many weak spots like us".

He said pointing to different areas on the board.

"What we have found that works is blessed ammo, Preach says a prayer over them and it burns and does more damage plus they hate it and makes them drop their vale for all to see".
George said.
"So we could drop the vale in front of witnesses then, that way all could see what is really going on".
Adam Watts said.
"Yes it would be a great idea but it would cause city wide panic, and alert them to our presents and we would be shut down, secrets are our strength for now".
George said then continued with his tutorial.
"They have very hardened bones, thick skin and long reach, we found that fire is very effective but they are also very agile and fast. I won't lie we have lost many in obtaining this information".
George said sadly they broke for lunch giving everyone time to rest and let it all sink in and discuss it among them.
"I've seen the Dweller in action they almost feared him and he saved my life".

Tom said.
"The fair ones are strong and the workers they are just far tougher than us humans we need more of them fighting with us, but other than Ithilli they just don't like us that much".
Preacher said.
"We need to reach the source. Find the leader or boss".
Adam Watts said.
"They have way too much power with their people in high places, were stuck with just killing a hand full at night, and there seems to be more we can't keep up".
Tom said.
"Seeing them is not enough now".
Preacher said they ate but could not come up with anything going round in circles. they did more training for the rest of the day and were very exhausted Adam could not remember been this tired and dropped onto his bed aching but at the same time it felt great getting into shape and the food was great to he was not looking forwards to facing one of those things it was ok seeing it from a distance which was frightening enough it made him shiver just thinking

about it, he liked the people he was working with better than when he was a constable.

*

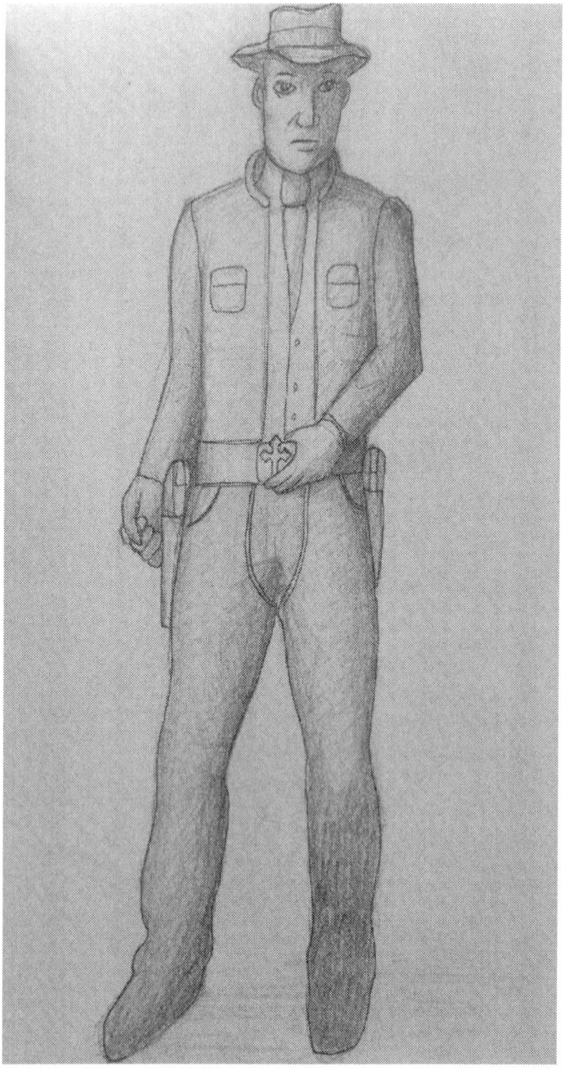

Henry John Longsfield smelt the sea air he could see England, the messages had been sent and his acolytes would rise from their slumber he knew God was his strength in this fight, the Fair Ones were demons hiding amongst them whispering their lies and deceit, not only were they poisoning the minds of the innocent but the very air they breathed. they were the spawn of the fallen, offspring of the Watchers and he wanted to wash them away once more and like Noah take with him those worthy and rise cleaned to never again transgress with no impurity or pride to be humble and possess prudence and then they shall be rewarded. Henry looked down to see his fists were clenched and white, but before he could do his mission from God one more of the Laurence family stood in his way, and she would have to be removed and then there one another to be punished, a defecator Matthew King. he patted the twin revolvers at his hips it was a time for justice Texan style, then pulled down the brim of his cowboy hat it was a hot day and bright too, he was a plain looking man nothing stood out, slim build greying hair, brown sharp eyes that hid the darkness with in, a force to be reckoned with.

Henry John Longsfield entered the office of Peter Aldward the man was weak and overweight, but had a keen business mind having already procured contracts overseas, using the Fair Ones, yes Henry wanted them gone but he was not stupid, he wanted to take everything from them, take them down. Show the whole world they had evil walking amongst them.
"Have the others awoken yet Brother Aldwark, i want to hold a meeting, find me that Laurence girl and Matthew King, she will not escape me this time".
"Yes sir, she has been seen poking her nose in and questioning the Fair Ones, she is being followed and watched as we speak".
"Very Good, and the other".
"He is a lot harder to track the last time he was seen was with that Stephenson fellow, he helps them hunt the dark ones, and has a church in the city centre".
"Well done brother, keep me posted, I wish to meet one of these Fair Ones too".
"Very well sir, I will see what I can do".

"There's no I will see, get it done, you answer to me first and no other than the Lord of the Spirits himself".

Aldwark stuttered yes, it made Henry sick, but he was needed because of his contacts, once their usefulness was at an end then those of a weak mind would also be cleansed and judged. He left the weak business man's office and took to the streets; he took an instant dislike to him. The city was too small, with tiny alleyways and roads, he felt penned in, the buildings seemed to lean over him, the air stank of smoke, the clothes that the people wore looked old and tatty, the weather changed too frequently, one minute it was hot the next it rained, he hated England only after one day. A room had already been booked so he checked in, the place was big and looked more like the taste he was accustomed to, but the room was too small as was the bed which was too hard. Henry was not happy at all but he knew this had to be handled personal and was too delicate for some laky sleeper.

He came from nothing having worked on his father's ranch, he attended church but he remembered wanting more, a thirst for knowledge and took up the priesthood, studied religious history, but it was not enough until he found part of an ancient text the book of Enoch, it switched on something inside him, it spoke to him, as if it was fate that he should find it, but he became obsessed finding out everything he could, but others wanted it too. Then one man made a breakthrough claiming to have translated it all to English. Henry told all it was fake to only steal it for himself, the church did not approve but by then he thought himself above even them. He saw them as weak and decadent, trapped in the past having lost their power and influence. He began his own crusade teaching others and soon had a following which grew and grew. He began to see the parables and metaphor everywhere, seeing himself as the Ram amongst the sheep, a King and making them his own, his followers would hang off his every word, gaining members spreading his words, other groups formed, his sleepers were in high places such as the law and governments, the rich and people with power and influence.

*

Rathan Stone wanted to spread further afield to expand, he liked the humans knew they were not perfect but neither were his own people. He did not like how they were treating them and using them like slaves, they had feelings and had potential, he saw the bond of love they had for each other and family was important, he only wanted what was best for them, he saw Ithilli working with the poor and even their own workers were treated badly, she did a lot of good work, did not mind getting dirty, the elders were so far up themselves now, decadent, acting like royalty and were no better than the workers or humans. Then there was the beautiful Marlitho Thornbrook one of the high members she made him feel young again unearthing long dead feelings that he had long buried deep down since leaving their homeland, it saddened him to see the beauty fade and withered, to see the corruption, and they

had all lost family and loved ones. The Earth plane was a way to start again some had even taken human partners, but Rathan knew they were just running from their past and it was not something his people could run from, the elders turned a blind eye to the evil that walked among them, Marlitho was different and like-minded he found her on the city walls where she often walked, she gave him a warm smile her long red hair shone in the sunlight.
"You look stunning today my lady".
"Well thank you Rathan".
He could tell she was preoccupied.
"You always brighten my day, but things are not running very smoothly of late, production is down, our workers and humans are afraid".
She said and he told her of his plan involving Edward Ludlam and Peter Aldwark, their expansion and export, but this did not seem to please her, it had been her work and planning to get the humans to work for them, give them their technology, Rathan had seen a change in her lately a cloud and it's shadow had been cast over her, and hated to see her this way, they

went back along way he knew her past and the great love she had lost, he knew there was no way to fill that void, when the Fair took a mate it was for life they were monogamous, they lived for thousands of years. If only he could crack the ice in her heart, having lost his own beloved who had been one of their worker Cast, which was also frowned upon, the corruption had eaten away at her once strong body and then her mind. So the two had found each other, with their broken hearts.

"Thank you for that and your support Rathan, I knew we have help each other throughout these rough times and I knew things will get better soon, you will see as will all".

She said but Rathan was not quite sure about that last part, he did worry about her and the mood swings, quick to anger. But he would just be there and on her good days he saw the old Marlitho, she had such inner turmoil and bitterness. She stared out over the city, he wanted to hold her tell her how much he cared and wanted to take it all away from her to shoulder the burden and be her rock.

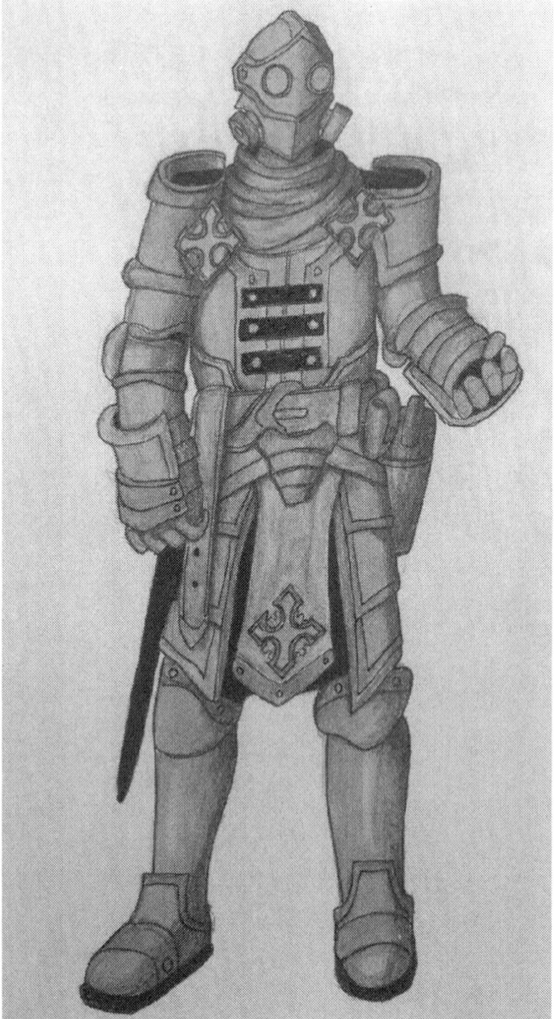

*

The next day the suits were brought out for Tom, Adam and Richard. "We're going on a mission tonight".
Tom said but sounded very enthusiastic it was then that George came to them.
"I want Adam ready; show him the ropes, so he can see what we are up against".
George said, Adam felt nervous having only seen one and from a distance so did not knew what to really expect, being a constable was not hard they had to be fit, able bodied and tall, no real fighting skills were required so to be show techniques was good and nice to learn but putting it in to real life action was another thing altogether.
"Don't worry it's just a patrol, I'll show you the ropes".
Tom said he seemed younger than them but more experienced and looked like he had been through a lot but Adam felt confident enough with him along. They were helped into their suits and used a simple assault course so they grew

accustomed to it and the weight, it was difficult to move and cumbersome, Adam grew hot very quickly. Tom flew across it as did big Richard. Then they went over to the shooting range.

"A body shot works best, the ancient blessed ammo will burn them, they will drop their Vale, I've only ever wounded them".

Tom said, they took a break and took off the suits again and it was such a relief he felt all light again but it was necessary, they were shown what their claws did to metal, an old suit design was shown to him, it was almost like an ancient suit of armour from the days of Knights, George had taken parts of the design and incorporated into his own, having seen the damage done to metal he did not what to imagine what they could do to flesh, they ate a late lunch and chatted, the weather was warm and sunny Adam could not believe that such evil and darkness was happening all around them he kind of wished he could go back to not know, ignorance was bliss he thought.

"So how did you meet George, and end up doing this".

Adam asked Tom.

"I stole from him actually and was living rough at the time, but he told me he believes in second chances and took me in, at first I just fetched and carried then grew from there I guess".

Tom said just finishing a plow man's pickle sandwich and got it on the corner of his mouth.

"And what about you Richard".

Adam asked. He was eating a ham sandwich but the meat slices were massive with almost half a pig in there, the man had an appetite.

"George had been putting himself through night school and working days with his father at the pit, I just kept seeing him and we got talking about wrestling and his inventing, and have known each other since, he just called me in and showed me that coloured lens and the rest you know".

The big man said then promptly belched loudly and it echoed much to the disgust of the others around them.

"It's the same story for most around here, George just takes in us waifs and strays everyone knows him as the father of steam,

but we know more and the double life he leads, if only they knew hey".
Tom said and they all agreed.

What little was left of that sunny day Adam had a dark feeling it would be awhile before such days would return they spent it laying around he wandered the grounds and drank iced lemonade, and was making the most of it until they were called back in and had to suit up once more, it was hot inside and the cool evening only help a little, they boarded a coach and the three were taken back into York entering through Monkgate Bar, it was just getting dark and close to dusk, none payed them any heed, they could see the Minster from there, it was where Tom was taking them, the Smog had rolled in thick but with their suits on they did not have to breath it in, the three entered a narrow cobbled street which brought them out the east side of the huge building, it made Adams stomach feel funny just looking up at it he was not that great with heights. Nobody was about, all was quiet. Tom lead the way then he darted forward, Adam got turned around in the mist, then bugs landed on him and the lens, it was hard to see in the suit and found himself alone, he called out to Tom and Richard but trying not to be too loud, it came out a muffled loud whisper sound, he turned on the suits little lamplight, it ran on a small battery at his belt which also powered a fan to keep the suit cooled and filtered the air too. His light just glared back at him he put his hand to the ancient stone and followed it round in the general direction the young lad had taken, he heard a shuffle and movement but something big came at him from the side knocking him against the wall hard and robbing the breath from his lunges, one of the lenses fell out but he saw what had attacked he saw it as a fair One and the twisted version at the same time this one seemed worse all angry, he pulled his revolver out but it was clawed from his grip and moved in close its bad breath stung his exposed eye, it was truly fast and even worse this close up, Adam kicked it back but he might as well have kicked the Minster's wall for what good it did, he throw a punch with his metal gauntlet fist and managed to connect, this made the creature take a step back, adrenaline rushed through him, he grabbed the side arm and managed to fire off a shot which clipped it as it disappeared into the mist with a howl, here he found the others they too had been attacked and looked like they had not fared any better than him.

"That was strange their not usually so organised or work in groups like that, we should leave and warn George".

Tom said. The three made their way back to Monkgate to await their ride back, it was starting to have been a long time and was worrying the young lad, they stepped out from under the walls, figures came out of the Smog out numbering them, the horse and carriage arrived fast the horse reared up and kick one down and knocked another down then the door swung open it was Jillith, the three wasted no time and jumped in, one grabbed the door, Richard used his size twelve boot and sent the monster flying, they were soon speeding away bouncing around in the back, once the city was behind them the carriage slowed heading down the gravel driveway.

Adam was tried and could not wait to remove the suit then headed straight for George who was in his office with Tom and Richard.
"You could have got us killed tonight; it looked like they were onto us".
Adam said and was angry.
"He's right George, we were lucky tonight, they were waiting for us".
Tom agreed with Adam.
"Then we need better weapons or more training maybe or bigger a patrol".
George said but even he knew they would have to change tactics not wanting to lose more people.
"Get some rest you three, leave it with me for now, and we'll talk more in the morning".
George ordered them out. Adam headed to his room it took a while for him to sleep, still on edge after his first real encounter knowing they wound be waiting in his dreams so he thought about Ithilli and smiled.

*

Ithilli Norium liked the humans and could not understand why her own people hated them yet were here helping it never felt right to her, she used the lens on her own people she did not have a high access and was looked down upon for helping the poor and sick humans their own workers were not treated much better, she had to find out what was going on and if this had happened before after hearing from Lucy and her book, her mother was ancient and wise oh and a little kooky too, anybody else would not like her pocking around, the Dweller too seemed familiar there were many old stories, she lived out in the country and mostly kept to herself, Ithilli found her in an old run down cottage that was over grow with weeds still in the same place and had not changed a bit and knew she was there even before she entered.
"You finally came to see your old mother". She said in a croaky voice hunched over her beauty long gone wizened and full of wrinkles but still a brightness in her eyes.
"What is it this time dear".

She always made out that's what she came for which was not true well maybe not in the last hundred years anyway.

"There are evil ones among us and are using the vale magic".

Ithilli said.

"Then you have a dark Dryad among you, pulling the strings".

The older Fair One said.

"A what now".

"You spend far too much time with those weak minded humans".

"We have become too complacent and decadent mother, the evil is killing both our kind and the humans they have found a way to see them, were all in danger".

Ithilli said.

"Stop been so dramatic child, how have you forgotten our history and where we came from".

The truth was she had.

"As you should well know we were once known as the first Folk a union with a dryad brought about what we are today our beauty was second to none, our power and strength there will always be those jealous one of our own who was corrupt called

Luthano Rockheart he tried a union but he corrupted the tree spirit and the offspring were called the Wrong who were shunned we fought in a great battle and they were beaten and banished and Luthano Rockheart disappeared".
The old one said.
"So he is back then and trying to free them".
Ithilli said.
"Yes but if it is him and he tries to free the Wrong from their banishment he will be unleashing every evil there ever was and is to be will fall upon our world, you must seek the original corrupt dryad only she will know how to stop him and what he seeks to do".
Her mother said Ithilli did not know what to do or think she needed to tell the others even if it meant telling them their secrets which she would not be allowed to do and decided she did not need to tell them everything.
"There is one more thing mother, a mixed Fair One they call the Dweller, he is like no other I've seen he feels old ancient even but knows nothing of himself or past".

Ithilli said but could see it was all taking its toll on her mother as if the past was too much for her to bear.

"There are so many things out there; he could be from the great battle or some accident".

She was tired now and looked frailer to her than ever before and knew it was time to leave.

"Thank you mother you have shed some light on this problem, rest now, I will visit you again soon".

"You better do young one, I won't always be here you know".

"You will be here long after us all".

They said their goodbyes and kissed her on the forehead it was like dry wrinkled paper Ithilli felt sad as she headed back to the city needing to find the Fair One responsible but the history lesson had only brought with it more questions but more then she knew earlier her mother had been holding back more too so decided to ask around her superiors did not know the name or anything about the story and just said that her mother was crazy any way but she suspected they were lying the way they looked as if nervous and should not even mention it, even the older ones seem to refuse to have anything to do with it, so she made her way back to the Hall she would have to reveal some to them and would have to take them to her world it no longer had its beauty no lush fields or ancient oaks that reached way up into the sky, fluff seeds blowing on the warm breeze, the smells and the colours now it was just twisted and dead it started after the great battle way before her time, pieces of the land were just black and rotten the once beautiful beasts and creatures were now foul and evil so they had to leave their world behind and once more help the humans like they did centuries ago, many found the life good and liked the humans such as the Workers but the more ancient Fair Ones were still stuck in the old ways disliking change and the humans too, but Ithilli grow to like them they had their faults but so did her own who thought themselves above them yet still had the same problems with love, power struggles and hatred but with them living for so long such things as love were difficult if it went wrong they were monogamists so finding a life mate was hard too, Ithilli had yet to find hers she did not like the way her people were heading so decadent and full of resentment no longer seeing beauty in things and pessimistic all the time so for now she had turned her back to trying to find love to helping the poor, needy and unwanted giving them food and medicines finding them work in the factories and workshops getting more houses built so for this they gave it to her as a job a liaison between them so they did not have to see or be seen with them which suited her just fine and with less time spent with her own she hated pretending just so she could fit in, they hated change just as much as the humans did, they were trying so hard to be above and different from them they became more like them it made her mad and laugh at the same time.

Ithilli took a coach and soon arrived, Adam and the gang looked tired George had been pushing them hard the man did not want to lose any more but they would never be strong enough to fight them if there was more than one her own people would not lift a finger and not care if the humans were been taken but she cared and admired his hope and tenacity and stubbornness she like humans for this they could be capable of so much and just had to believe in themselves. Then there was Adam Watts he was immune to their Fair charm and so saw them for what they were she could see him struggle with it he was a lot like Sarah the seer but what they were going through only made them stronger, first she would have to speak with George and he would not like her taking his students away.

*

Adam Watts had finished eating with the others when they heard George arguing with Ithilli they entered the dining area she wanted to take all of them and he was having none of it, then she said three and that was fine but when it came to choosing who, they started arguing again in the end it was Tom, Sarah who had come out of her shell a lot more and even trained with them the last was Adam he did not mind having a break from training she came over to them. "You three will be accompanying me on a mission of great importance and it could be dangerous, will you do this there is much we could learn".

The three could do nothing but agree if it helped with what they were doing, George moaned about it but he too could see that it made sense and besides that she could be very persuasive, they were to set off first thing in the morning when she would return and so with that she was gone, the Fair one smelt so good to Adam, it hurt his head just thinking about her too and to go on a mission with her sounded good to him.

After eating they would have a down time were they would read or listen to George and his tall stories and tales the things he had invented and his outlandish ideas a place called the Hollow Earth, the George lamp that help miners when they hit a gas pocket so unlike normal lamps that would catch fire so his idea was safer having worked there himself and just wanting his father to be safe and his fellow workers his ideas were on par with the Fair Ones at times, then there was his baby the locomotive he was working on he said it would revolutionise the world some day in his usual booming northerner accent he was so likeable though, then they dragged their tired selves to bed ready to ach in the morning then to start all over again. The armour had been worked on since and they had been training in it too, it no longer steaming up the lenses, more moveable but not much lighter, they were to be using it on their mission not that she was giving much away about the details.

*

Lucy woke with a start and knew right away she was not along in the dark room and hoped it was the ghost, the lamp came on it was a young man pointing a revolver at her with rope too.
"You're coming with me, Henry requires a meeting, but as you can see you have no choice".
He said Lucy was still in the narrow bed and as he came closer she kicked the weapon

out of his hand it went off putting a hole in the ceiling above the pare, she grabbed the loose bed sheet and throw it over his head and face and shoved him to one side and made a run for the door, but he recovered quickly and grabbed her wrist as she pulled the door open, his grip was strong, this time with her free hand she punched him as hard as she could but it did not do much other than anger him, he gave her a back hand, Lucy hit the floor hard knocking the wind out of her and then the world went dark.

When Lucy woke again she was in a dark room tied to a chair a familiar figure stood before her cowboy hat and all.
"Well we meet again, these Fair Ones won't protect you, I am the Elect we see and know all, and all shall fall before me, and will lay waste to all who stand in my way, you shall burn in the white fires of the Lord of the spirits.
"You know your problem Longsfield... You talk far too much, they are already onto you, and I have also warned them".
"This does not matter, we are legion one falls two will rise".

He said.

"Why are you holding me, you have all but destroyed my family, there is nothing to gain".

"It's not you I want my dear". But even before he finished she know "like a sheep he will come running to me, I could have taken you anytime you are just bait".

"He means nothing to me, he won't fall for it, you on the other hand hate that he left that all so powerful cult, that's all it is, you are all crazy zealots, you pray on the weak, giving them hollow promises, following some fake non cannon manuscript".

She said baiting him on purpose, and it was working.

"I don't need you awake or even alive for him to come back to his brethren. You and your father are the fakes in all of this. I will be rewarded and ascend, I will be at his side, Angels will weep".

"You are delusional, you twist what is written to your own agenda, making it sound like your own words, your interpretations are wrong and negative, do you actually know what parables and metaphors, what you preach are just lies, and falsehood, it's your own fears you deny, your own greed and hatred are what you serve".

She said and he stepped in and slapped her across the face she could taste blood. But knew she had hit a raw nerve with just her words.

"When the time comes you will be begging me for mercy".

"What, after you have beaten me some more, does it make you feel like a man, you spout the rules but don't follow them yourself, I can add hypocrite to my list now, this is not how the Elect were or would want to be portrayed, you are making a mockery of them".

"Enough bitch, I grow tired of that serpent tongue of yours or I will have it remove, the bait doesn't need to be whole".

He said and she knew all that he was a bully, a liar and weak, he only knew violence and terror. Longsfield left her to her thoughts she tried the bonds but it was too tight and tied well but the chair creaked and wobbled a little, it was weak.

*

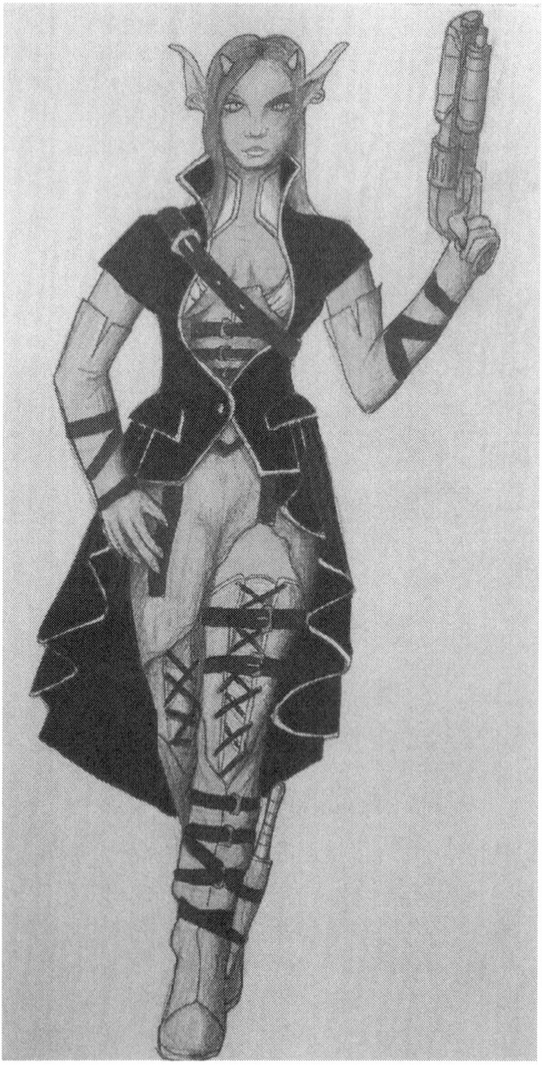

The next morning they were up had breakfast and started to suit up when Ithilli returned she was dressed in a light leather armour a long jacket and thigh boots a small thin sword at her hip and a cross bow on her back, red flame hair tied back which made her look very stern and deadly serious in fact she did not say much and seemed to be in a foul mood which was not like her at all, she got them on a large wagon and drove it herself they would need to leave unnoticed because of the way they were dressed it would arouse suspicion and she was very eager to go, it was still early morning and cold, the days had been hot of late so the cool morning air was a welcome with the suits on to, the ride was hard and bumpy and she was still not very forthcoming again with the details, the four were soon out in the countryside and it was a nice change it was midday when the wagon finally stopped so they could get out to stretch and walk a little Ithilli told them they were close to a place called Brennen rocks it was an odd place with its strangely weathered rocks which had formed them

into strange formations and shapes there was no other place like it, scientists had studied it but it was just natural but to the Fair Ones it was sacred they made their way through it was abundant with of wildlife, plants and trees and could be a nice place to visit it seemed odd but then he was getting used to that she brought them to a rock it was massive and seemed to stand away from the rest the thing looked like a giant turnip with its base weathered away to the point it looked like it might fall.
"We are here, when I put my hand on it, step through".

She said leaving them totally confused as to what she was talking, about she sighed and told them to just do it, Adam stepped up first he trusted her she place her hand on the stone the air in front of him seemed to shimmer like a road on a hot day he took a step forward then was faced by complete darkness and dizziness before falling to his knees and knew straight away he was no long in Yorkshire, he wiped the lenses and blinked what was before him was a Barren wasteland bear with patches of brown long dead grass, it was cold with a low mist, the

sky dull and grey, he waited for a long time
and still the others had not arrived he was
starting to worry, he waited longer that was
when he heard a strange noise a wailing
which made him shiver and knew
something was coming a shadow in the
distance he thought it might have been the
others but the moan came again this time
closer then it seemed all around and eating
at his mind, he ran and came to what
looked like trees from a distance but on
getting closer they were dead and black the
branches were like clawed hands many
were fallen the thing was getting closer so
he hide inside one of the huge dead trees
and looked like it my smell bad but thanks
to George's improvements it hand its own
air filter which kept the lenses fogging over
he held the hand cannon very afraid and
just hoped it would pass him by.

*

Tom landed hard in a river of the black
sludge, it was sticky like tar making it hard
for him to swim/crawl out, once out he had
to lay on the river bank to catch his breath,

it was all over the suit and looked like it was going to be hard to remove, he stood shaking it off his boots then took in his surroundings the other two were not with him he was starting to regret coming here he was younger than the others with more to prove because of his age and throw himself in to the jobs and patrols but that did not mean he was any less fearless, he looked up to George the big man was like a father to him, nobody had trusted Tom or treated him with respect, he never knew his parents and escaped the terrible orphanage, living rough, stealing food and whatever he could to survive and so he did not want to let George down and end up back in his former life or existence.

Tom waited longer but grow uneasy like he was not alone, he moved away from the black river but did not know which direction to go but just knew to keep moving was best, a swarm of bugs came from nowhere and were on him some had no choice and stuck to the black tar, they could not penetrate the suit they were black their wings came out of a shell on the back the front was the nasty end it was all mandibles and teeth, he waved his arms around trying to fed them off but they would not leave him alone, he saw what looked like a forest in the distance and he ran that way hoping for cover and out run the cloud of teeth. Not that the forest looked like and more inviting, the trees looked evil with branches that looked more like claws, here the bugs left him alone, he picked his way through the many threes and dying bushes which many had thrones, exposed roots and uneven ground made it worse to walk, as Tom moved deep he saw movement out of the corner of his eye but just thought it was the masks lens, a branch snagged on his suit but as he pulled free it seemed to come to life and began rapping around his leg at first then more grabbed at him, he tried to make a run for it but fell where more wrapped around him and then was dragged he screamed then passed out.

*

Sarah was not doing any better than Tom and Adam having appeared on high ground having fallen hard on her backside, she walked over to a cliff edge to try and get her bearings but could not see the other two, there was a wide valley with dead trees that stretched far into the distance. The ground gave way beneath her and she dropped and rolled down for a long time and finally came to a sudden stop the suit had taken most of the fall but she was shaken up, the lens had a crack and there were dents and scratches she had lost her pack and had to retrieve her side arms and dusted them off. Sarah heard movement and saw what looked like a horse she blinked and cleaned the lens of dust then her heart all but stopped it was a unicorn her first unicorn it was a massive beast but looked ill and on seeing her it bolted, she had read stories about them reading was all she had but to see one was like a little girls dream come true, she heard more galloping and turned to it hoping the beast of myth had returned, but was met by another creature of Myth.

*

George sat up in his bed Jillith moaned next to him but stayed asleep he knew something was wrong so slipped on his robe and headed down stairs, grabbed a lamp lit it but the light glared back at him in the darkness on reaching the bottom he slipped at the bottom and fell back there was a thick liquid, it was blood and the front door was open cool night air chilled him but it was not that making him shiver across the lawn ran what looked like hundreds of people all heading his way and fast but there was something wrong about them the way they seemed to stumble and fall over each other, footsteps joined him it was Richard he was half dressed and half asleep.
"Your popular tonight, but maybe we should close the door".
Richard said. He did not have to tell him twice he locked it as the crowd reached the paved patio they hit the door hard but it held for now, they clawed at the glass with blooded hands and a crazed look in their

eyes moaning and growling and trying to get in.
"What the hell is going on".
Richard said.
"I don't know but there is more were not alone in here".
And as George spoke there was a scream from upstairs, it was jillith he ran taking the steps two at a time Richard headed to his room to grab his gear.
George entered his room to find Jillith grappling with one of the people and was finding it hard when normally she would of thrown him across the room he ran in and it the man hard using his best wrestling move cloth lining him off her there was blood on her neck but seems fine otherwise.
"Who is he and what's going on George?"
"I wish I knew my sweetheart, but there's more outside and are after our blood".
He said and she wiped her neck.
"He bit me, and bloody strong too".
She said the downed man moaned and got back up this time coming at George, he kicked him back but he just kept coming jillith hit the man hard in the head with the bedside lamp he went down with a

smashed skull and did not move after that and she could hit hard and he had played wrestled with her before so knew first hand and more and more besides.

Weapons fire came from downstairs startling them, he grabbed the shot gun he had under the bed she grabbed the lamp and the headed out onto the landing to find Richard running up to them.

"There are far too many and must have come in somewhere else, we need to reach the workshop".

It was a sound plan and the three headed that way using the back servant staircase which would bring them down to the kitchen then went out in to the court yard it was empty they ran past the horse stalls to the workshop once inside they bolted the door here they suited and armoured up it gave them a breather and time to try and get their head around what was going on, this was why George did not want to split them up for Ithilli's whim of a mission.

"They just don't stay down".

Richard said.

"Smack em in the head".

Jillith said George's accent was catching.

"We need a plan, and we need to know what we are up against here".
As they were getting ready Jillith moaned and had to sit down.
"I don't feel so good Gee".
She said, Gee was her pet name for him, he went to her side and held her strong rough hand it was cold and clammy in his, her head was hot like she was running a fever, then without warning began to fit shaking then lay still he stayed at her side her body was cold as if she were dead he shock her, called her name, then she moved but she was no longer his beloved and she went for his throat but his suit stopped her he had to jump back and called her name again but it was like she did not hear him and like the man in their room was not going to be stopped but he could just not do that to her.
"I don't think I could do it, locker her up for now mate".
Richard said.
"She had no pulse she was dead and still is, it would be putting her out of her misery, I will do it".

George said and grabbed the lamp she had used then let her get close then hit her hard with one hit she went down and stayed there he knelt beside her and covered her up a tear dropped onto the oily sheet he grabbed his shotgun loaded put on his suit helmet whoever it was responsible for this was going to pay there would be a time for morning now was the time for justice.
The two were ready and headed outside, workers and hall hands were running around screaming and panicking Richard turned his Gatling gun on the mass of undead Ones exploding heads with perfect accrues but it did not seem to make a difference they kept coming as they got closer George went into a rage blasting them with his shotgun and when that ran out of ammo he used it to smash heads and seemed unstoppable he just kept seeing Jillith her smile and when they had first met they had worked hard together and it just happened between them they fell in love he had never known such a connection he still could not believe she had been taking from him tears blurred his eyes then the next moment Richard was shaking him out of his

zone he looked back and just saw body's in his wake they were all gone a tiredness took over him and he knelt in the blood and gore and let out a cry of despair, Richard stood over him George finally stood and walked away he stayed back giving the man some space they went back to the workshop reloaded and were ready once more as dawn broke it was then they saw the true extent of the carnage and death George sat on the steps looking out over it all, helmet beside him staring out feeling cold and empty oh they were going to pay big.

5

Edward ludlam loved his new job and the trouble he was causing, the workers were on strike with fighting in the streets overwhelming the constables and the justice of the peace, it was all going to plan and he marched at the head of them down Parliament Street with pride taking it to them, they love him for it the law could not touch him now no more weaving in a factory for him, as they marched something seemed wrong it was as if the air shimmered around them some of them dropped as if fainting then everybody was doing it dropping like flies then fitting on the ground Edward panicked and instead of helping he ran to the side of the road heard screams as these that had dropped got straight back up but they were different somehow, then all hell broke loose as they turned on those that were stood watching and confused then were attacked, tearing at their throats who then went down then were soon back up joining the ranks. Edward ran from their leaving behind the pleas for help and screams of terror, this was not what he had in mind and made his way to the office of the Fair Ones but they were either gone or would not answer the door then from nowhere one of the fainters came at him, the women's fine dress was torn and blood soaked she was pretty but was after him trying to bite at his throat he managed to pull her off but she would not stop even when he shouted at her, then punched her hard but that did nothing to slow her down either more came on hearing the two struggling, Edward pulled away and made a run for it down Davygate, how could such a thin happen he thought the city centre had many small churches so he ran into one now and blotted the heavy door but he was not alone there were people who had the same idea it seemed a logical thing they were strong buildings high windows, strong doors nothing to do with the religion of the places they looked afraid and so was he and they did not look any happier to see him he sat in one of the pews and jumped as the door was hammered on with screams for help and the fainters trying to get in with him was a family and some randomers he wanted to wait this out until they had moved on away from the door and told them to be quiet, the children were afraid and started crying. This quiet time gave him chance to think having never seen such horror and gore or why they were all acting that way it was like a switch had been flipped how happy he had felt it had all turned into hell.

*

Adam Watts left the rotten hole in the tree and walked through the petrified forest trying to avoid the thick black oozy mud, a thudding sound stopped him in his tracks it sounded like heavy foot falls then he heard a scream a very human one he entered a clearing and saw Sarah surrounded by what looked like a type of horse but with a human torso a twisted version of a centaurs they looked sick and corrupted with boils and sores on their bodies, they were armed with log spears Sarah had two revolves but the three just soaked up the bullets and was having no effect on them, Adam fired at one and got their attention even his weapon had little or no effect then more came these seemed in worse state with twisted limbs bent in the wrong direction they shuffled and limped shambling to them they were surrounded one that seemed less afflicted approached them.
"You have safe passage to our lady and no harm will come to you".

It said and all they could do was be lead deeper into the forest and it was getting dark the whole place hurt his head and was making it ach, Sarah was not taking it all too well she had not trained that much with them or a suit on even though hers had been altered and slimed down he just hoped she would keep it together when they reached their destination, stood before them was a massive oak tree but it was just as dead and rotten as the rest its branches clawing into the sky with more black ooze everywhere he hoped Ithilli and Tom were ok, a figure seemed to materialize out of the tree it was female the dark Dryad.

"More humans are you joining or fighting me, as for stopping me your too late because you little visit was just what I needed".

The Dryad said, she was a mixture of a beautiful woman or maiden Fair one and beast pacing round the tree in a very provocative way.

"What she means is it was my fault when we entered my home world it opened the barrier between our worlds". Ithilli said as she joined them Tom was with her too they did not have their weapons either held at spear point.

"So thank you, you might want to run along home because your loved ones will die and rise again as an unstoppable army, but before you hate me it's directed at the wrong one this is only partly my doing, and whatever story you have been told is false and fed to you as a lie".

She said then leaned on the tree, Adam looked at Ithilli for any confirmation but she was just looking down at her feet.

"We were once one, a people but they soon turned on each other having everything does not bring you happiness they were greedy and began to kill each other that's where Luthano Rockheart comes in. we loved each other but it was never meant to be it was forbidden".

The dryad said and paced round but never leaving the tree.

"The split came and they all but killed each other, and I grow sick my beloved is the key to this you must find him before it is too late, this is all the help I can give, it is and has always been out of my hands, go back, for my sins all I can do is watch powerless, one among the Fair Ones is behind this, find these two".

She said looking sad.
"This is all my doing I was used, the Wrong are now free, it was all a dirty trick".
She said then told Adam to step closer away from the others. As he stood before him she was very tall and would have been very beautiful at one time now close up she looked tired and ill, warts and boils were breaking out on her once strong body, and bits of branches were growing out of her flesh.
"You have something about you human you see me and my people as they really are, and I like that about you, and you may need this in the battle to come".
She said sadly.
"How can we get back through without weakening the Vale even more".
Ithilli said.
"You must find the rift this side find where and how the Wrong are getting through, there is your way back".
The Dark Dryad said then turned back to Adam who was still stood next to her.
"She has feelings for you mortal one".
She said for only him to hear.

"I've grown weak and have little or no power here".

She said for all to hear then from the high branches Tom was lowered and released from the vine like grip and it was time to leave the Dryad stepped behind the tree and was gone leaving the four wondering what to do next Ithilli had not planned for this or to hear another side to the story but was not surprised by this and could only wonder at what else her people were holding back.

"So where to now".

Sarah said.

"We follow the corruption, which will be dangerous and see where it takes us, there are a few places of power where a rift could be formed and even maybe the very one we used to enter your world".

"It seems to me that one of your own is behind this but why".

Adam said.

"My people will not talk to each other about this, or anybody else for that matter like it is some big dark secret or conspiracy".

Ithilli said then they began to follow her leaving the forest or what was left of it, avoiding the beasts and anything else that looked nasty and she was been very quiet to Adam, Tom told them that the tree had just grabbed him and was thankful they had arrived when they did but seemed unharmed nonetheless. Ithilli took them past massive ruins and sacred places he could see her sadness could only wonder at how beautiful her world must have been then to see it slowly dying and wasting away, must be hard on her he thought and could see she did not want to talk about it, they did not linger and quickened their pace it would be dark again soon which worried him the way she was acting nowhere seemed safe there.

*

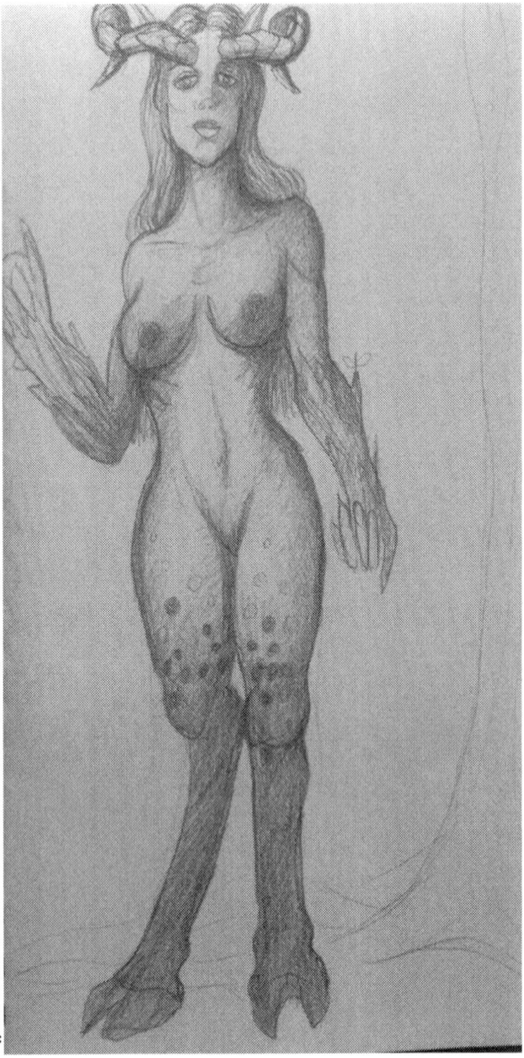

Matthew King(Preacher)or father King, had often thought of Lucy and wished thing could have been different and turned out better than just like that she was back in his life, knowing he had hurt her. She had not been in touch since her meeting the other day, Ithilli and Adam were still to return so could not get in contact with Lucy. He looked at the empty pews, his congregation grew less and less, the decline in numbers were due to what the fair Ones brought, he saw them all as demons with or without the lens yes they had brought Industrialization and urbanisation many had jobs there was money but he knew there was always a price, there were more poor and ill from the smoke and Smog, people were less God fearing now, once Bible was best and seeing God's hand everywhere, their minds were on other things like science now, going out to the coast, taking holidays and doing other things, and with the age of steam places were accessible, they still believed and would still go to church but he could see that their hearts just were not into it any more looking bored even, Matthew did what he could even going out to them, the families worked hard and long hours, he stayed away from the Fair Ones they did not believe in just one God, they were a lot like ancient man with Druids and Mother Earth, it was all nonsense to him and blasphemous.

The Church of England did not like what was happening and with Queen Victoria embracing the industrial revolution did not help matters. Matthew knew they would have to change and adapt they were going to lose everything, he knew how desperate and paranoid they could be, the influences they had and the dark times they had been through, he felt their pressure and knew how stubborn they were too, change did not happen quickly if at all.

Matthew King did what he could, to him it was a double edged sword, he saw good in the industrial revolution and what the Fair Ones had done, but they were moving too fast and many were falling behind, the church being one of them. Then he met George Stephenson the man made

Matthew see what was beyond, and that evil did walk among them, influencing those in power, people were going missing and found dead, the law did nothing but were just as corrupt and powerless, George asked him to join in the fight, Matthew knew a lot about religious history, less known and long forgotten texts and artefacts the Elect had shown him that and more. The two had debate late into the night on religion and science but in the end agreed to disagree, he had shown him the lens. Together they found the ancient word of God that was not supposed to be written down but if their weapons such as swords, blades and firearms

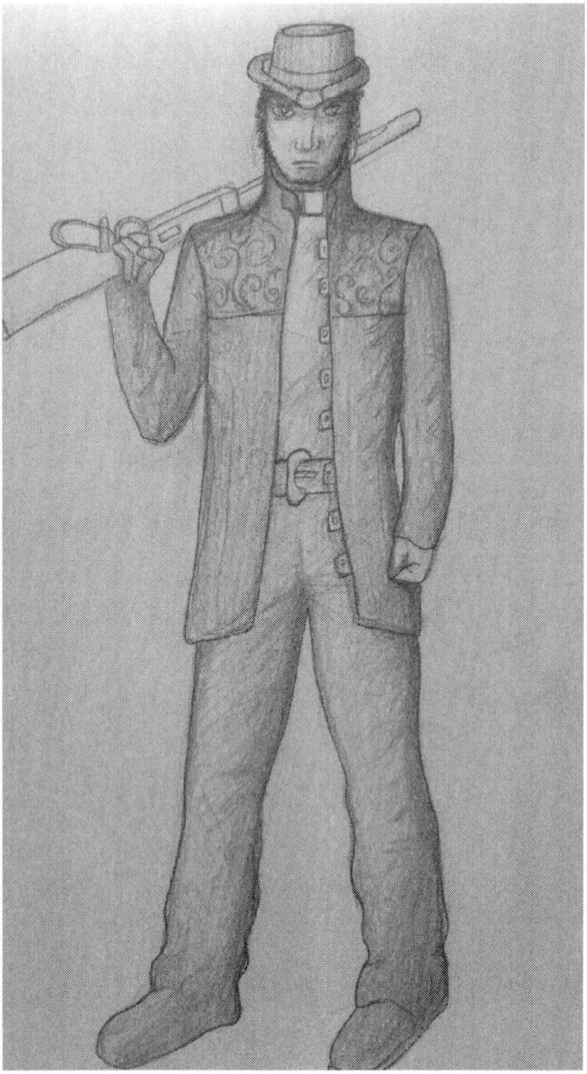

along with ammo could be blessed, it harmed the evil, even burning them. So Matthew jumped at the chance to be doing something instead of just standing idly by as the future came.

Matthew King heard a disturbance outside his church people rushed in panicking saying things how folk were just attacking one another, he used the tinted lens and saw bugs swarming around them and biting, those that dropped poisoned would rise again different and attack those around them, passing the poison on. He pulled inside the unaffected and bolted the heavy door trying to calm them down but he needed to get to George and quick, this was a new development, they were in danger and could not remain for too long, it had been a long time since the room was this full but there was no sermon today only survival, there were about five men but the rest were made up of women and children and all were crying shouting and talking over each other, so Matthew stepped up to his pulpit and slammed the huge old bible he kept there down hard, this made them all stop.

"We must be quiet or more poisoned ones will come, we cannot stay here, I have friends that can help us, but we must move fast, so help those around you, no panicking, we must work to together".

He told them. Then they started talking over each other again.

"Now is not the time to try and answer your questions, it is time for action".

He said then began delegating, the rowdy and panicked ones were to look out, the less noisy would help the younger children and carry if needed, then he lined them up and peered out, the poisoned ones had moved on, then he looked through his lens there were no bugs either, then Matthew opened it wider those who were look outs were sent a head then moved out along Davygate slowly at first, many left to return home and he did not stop them but told them to lock their doors and stay inside, he took who was left up Stonegate then Petergate the Minster was a head of them now, he wanted to get out of the narrow streets and the city, knowing they would stand a better chance in the open, he kept checking the lens then moved on.

*

George and Richard made it to his main workshop outside the city but even from there they could see how wide spread this was, there were a few fainters walking around but caused them little problems they kept out of there way they seemed to have bad eyesight and hearing too, it was in their numbers they became more of a danger.
"I've been working on something new, I call it the Walkermotive was going for Rocketwalker but that doesn't sound as good, maybe I'll use Rocket for the train version I have planned".
George said and opened the door what stood before them was an impossible machine and could only be described as a steam engine on legs and did not have wheels and would be free from tracks standing three meters tall with Gatling guns on either side a armoured compartment on

the front. The tall smoke stack at the back and long Pistons to drive the legs
"I'm going to contact a few associates of mine then mass produce them to fight this threat, then pull back to the city walls and defend ourselves".
George said.
"Wow that is a beast and a plan but will they help".
"Most likely not, they say I keep stealing their ideas but it's the other way around like my lamp idea".
"Will you let that one go already".
Richard said, they worked together to get the prototype ready and Richard climbed on board the controls were a little clunky using steam pressure to move the legs it was very slow but he soon got used to manoeuvring it around the lager workshop area and was very eager to give it a try on the fainters and the demons. George climbed on the back with it only been for one person they geared up and headed into the city centre stopping off at his associates homes showing them what he had made and that they needed to attend a meeting they cleared a way through, their next stop the

fair ones they caused quite a stir with the people and the constables but on seeing who it was and what his machine could do they let him pass and so all gathered in the Fair house George called them all together not caring how they all felt about each other, he told them of his plan to fortify the city against the hordes that were heading

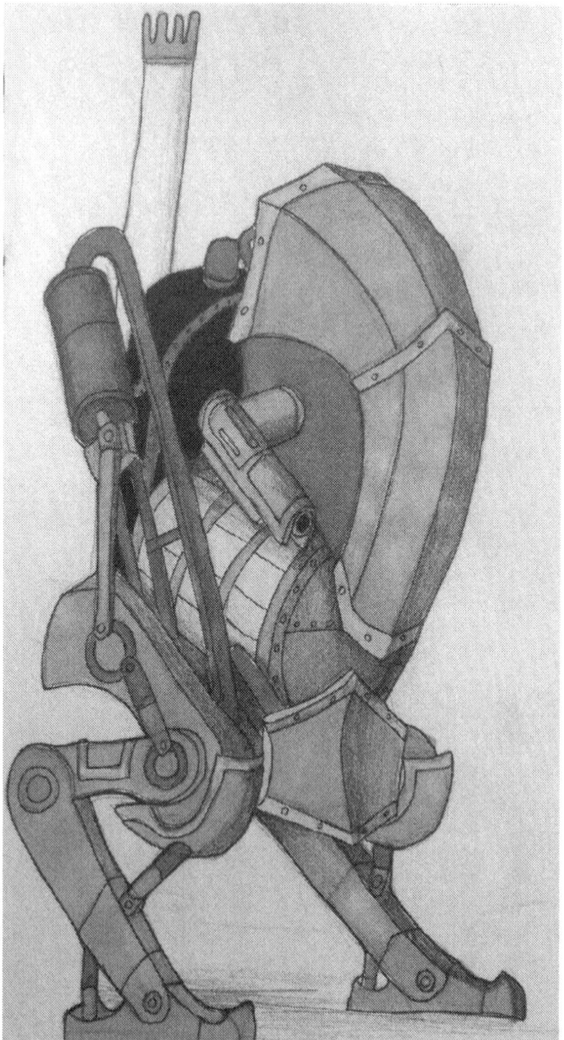

their way and there was little time in which to do so, government officials and heads of the fair ones did not like it at first George used the lens to see if there was any dark ones among them but since the Fainters they had made themselves very scares, he felt they were more than likely letting them do the work for them, they argued with each other putting the blame on the Fair Ones who denied it he could see that most of them did not have a clue what was going on anyway but he got through to them George's booming voice settled them back down.

"We need to pull together show those that want us divided that we can work together and survive this. I have special weapons and armour, plans to make more Walkermotives. Even lenses so you can see the demons that walks among us those responsible for the deaths of late, evil works all around us, but we have the tools, we are no longer blind".

His words got their attention, then the all started asking questions all at once.

"Right now we fight and defend our homes, block the roads and gates flush out the Fainters and evil".

They all liked his plan and he smiled wishing that Jillith was there, she said this would never happen, he was doing this for her it was like a part of him was missing she was so different from the other women, hardworking did not mind getting dirty and they would talk and laugh for hours she had been his soul mate now she was gone taken, turned into a mindless one and not only that but he had to kill her for mercy sake it had to have been him though. The meeting was at an end and work would start at first light, as they left Preacher appeared and looked a little worse for where having been missing most of the night he was glad to see him and told him about the unseen bug that were poisoning the people and described what he saw. There had no news about Ithilli or the others he needed them now more than ever, George was given a room to work from with a map of the city he grabbed pens and worked tirelessly through what was left of the night, marking all the routes and exits what would be used as barricades and finally feel asleep from exhaustion, Richard came to him in the morning he took the walkermotive so he could hold back the Fainters as they worked trams and cars were used doors from empty homes that were near and just about anything else that would help block any gaps, the work spread throughout the city, George went from one to the other helping them make them stronger it began to take hours and then days he worked tirelessly and would not be told even Richard dare not disturb him, he lost weight and looked tired and would not stop until people were safe.

6

Edward had done better than expected the rally had been a blood bath her plans were working chaos everywhere, but there was a thorn in her side a very big loud one, George Stephenson she would have to reach out to Edward again the Fainters as the humans had begun calling them would leave him be, she needed somebody on the inside who would keep her informed as to what they were up to or plans that they were up wind of she hated having to work with the humans there was lots to prepare for the Fainters were nothing compared to what was coming their weapons and barricades would not hold hell itself at bay for long, so for now she mingled in with her own people none knew who she was and so fitted in nicely tearing them apart from the inside it was all for Luthano he would return and be in her arms again he had started this so many years ago but had been exiled and punished for nothing but only because he was different but saw what his people were turning into but he had been put under a spell by the Dryad but she had taken care of her like the ancient one had told her to do now her offspring was the new army and this time they would not fail, next she would see her brethren fall starting with Ithilli, she had taken the humans with her to the fair realm and had played right into her hands, she had now started phase one having weakened the Vale and hopeful be stuck there or be another thorn in her side so goody goody helping the filthy humans she even smelled like them they made her sick, if they had not been so weak and needed the humans resources and would suck them dry and move on but this was the perfect time to strike then she could be killing two birds with one dark blow then she would have it all with her beloved Luthano at her side, she knew he had been exiled to the human realm but where, and they had also wiped his mind called, taking the forgotten. She had tried reaching out to him sent out her people nothing came back, it was frustrating, they knew what they were doing she was glad most of the elders were dead but one still remained Ithilli's mother she would get what she needed from her and end her too she had been slowly killing them all this would hurt Ithilli as well she wanted to hurt them, so they knew what loss would feel like how losing everything, she knew how Luthano felt now and why he had turned on his own because they were always after perfection, outdoing one another in childish games and if you did not fit in or looked like them then you were frowned upon, treated bad and kicked out.

Luthano had rebelled against this and many joined him he raised an army almost overnight of those who were different or deformed, a born leader and he won the heart of this new people he faced the Fair Ones, gave them a chance so they could still be as one but again they were shunned and spurned, she had fallen for him then but her advances were spurned too, the Dryad had turned his head she had promised him so much like they always do they were mermaids of the land all pretty but sirens of the forest and used him he did not listen to her or those around him but she did fill his ranks that would become the Wrong so if she could not have him nor would the dryad bitch that's when the Ancient Ones came to her and made their promises.

*

On the other side of the city up high in his bell tower sat the Dweller having seen the chaos and now George with his machines and barricades, he knew more was coming a feeling deep down but at the same time it felt familiar somehow and he could not shake that feeling his dreams too were becoming more vivid and remembered more and more his own passed remain allusive as ever though he saved the weak humans he could no longer sit idly, or hide away too it was time for action the others of George's group were missing then there was Ithilli she too seemed familiar to him like they had met before, it was late now and getting dark he would pay the inventor a visit first thing the man was becoming a leader as if he was born to be but looked tired his mate taken from him and was throwing himself into it all this the dweller or Smity has the big man called him could feel and see this they needed help and fast if only he could remember who he was, he slept but dreamt.

He stood tall and powerful his flesh smooth, hair blowing in the wind it smelt of a thousand body's and it was not a nice odour either he looked down at his hands they were not tipped by claws holding a mighty sword a thousand faced each other than a mighty horn was blown and the blood shed began, his forces were lower in number but what they lacked they made up in passion they were not the tall lethal Fair Ones with their shiny hair and armour all perfect and uniformed, his fighters were the shunned, different and ugly to them and so were feared so with that much hate and animosity thrown in more fell to their swords, it was brutal as he joined the fray killing and hurting, crushing who stood before him still more and more waves came he was covered head to toe in blood and gore a madness had taken over him a blind rage a berserker smashing armour cutting right through them his own stood aside as he killed a hundred as if nothing soon they would flee just at the sight of him, then the next day they would all line up again and the same would happen, it raged for days many fell on both sides and so he would once more take to the battle field and when his rage subsided he too saw what he had done, the deaths he had caused and so a truce was ordered and he stood before the elders.

The dweller awoke but only a feeling of guilt and fading images remained it was just beyond his grasp on the edge of his mind then it was gone like before it was frustrating. He dropped down and approached George he told him that Ithilli had taken Adam and the others and how he needed them back so the dweller(Smity) stepped in and began doing the heavy lifting pushing back the Fainters he proffered not to kill them and just knocked them down they were very strong and mindless turning who they bit into yet more filling their ranks who or whatever was behind this knew what they were doing and had to be stopped and so he help where he could and they were glad of the extra help there was no need for secrets and hiding now the constables were also helping but the Dark ones had gone like they knew this was going to happen he did not know if that was a good thing or not at least their influence was gone.

*

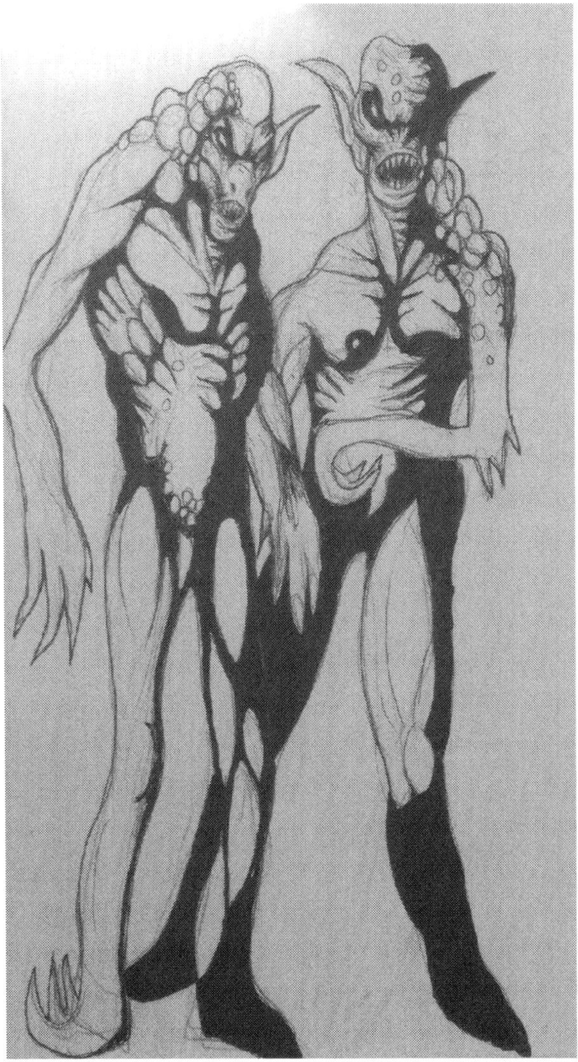

They rested, Adams feet hurt but Ithilli had been pushing them hard Sarah was not used to this much walking and was getting blisters so he approached her, she was been very quiet.

"So what is going on with you, Sarah is feeling it and so am I you are pushing us too hard".

He said when she finally stopped and she was not happy to be question either.

"We don't have time to rest and when we stop we are in danger".

She snapped at him again this was just not like her.

"Talk to me Ithilli, we can see something is bothering you, were your friends remember".

"You still call me friend after what I did, there may be nobody left to go back to, I might as well let them all through".

She said and he could see she was very upset.

"You weren't to know, you were tricked and manipulated like us all, we can make this right, but we will be no good to you tired".

He said and she seemed to calm a little and began to see what he was saying made sense, she nodded and gave them time to recover.

"Thank you Adam, I do now remember why I brought you, you see things differently and that's why I like you".

She said and her mood had lifted some more he remembered what the dryad had said about her liking him and it was something he was not about to go after yes she was very pretty to look at but it would just not work so he put that out of his mind and besides that she might of just been causing trouble and using them the Dark Dryad could not be trusted, he just hoped they could get back he did not like the place it felt like it was seeping into his very core it was making him ill and his headache, it was depressing just black mud and hills then more ruins then more dead trees it seemed never ending but Ithilli seemed to know where they were heading, so when they set off again the pace was a little slower but not by much and her mood was less snappy.

"I wonder what we will find there, and hopefully make some difference and stop it getting any worse".

Adam said trying to make light conversation and ease her mind some.

"I don't know, it makes me sick to see how this beautiful place has changed, I wish you could have seen it Adam, the beauty of your realm is only half of what it used to be, and I fear the say will happen to yours".

She said sadly Tom and Sarah had not said much he guessed it was too much to take in he could not believe how he was taking it so well just been a humble constable doing his beat now he was stood in another realm surround by such evil and deceit, he should just be running away and hiding but instead he took it in his stride which right now was squelching through black mud that seemed to sap his strength at every step. Ithilli stopped holding up her hand in a fist they followed her lead and ducked down low taking advantage of the hilly area in the distance stood a large Keep with high walls it looked half built but strong with what looked like Fair Ones yet were different they did not have the tall handsomeness

and beauty they limped and shuffled
instead of walked some were hunched over
they just had something wrong about them
wearing black twisted armour did not help
in their appearance either.

"Damn the standing stones are walled in
and guarded by the Wrong".

Ithilli said as they kept low Adam could see
the walls stretching far into the distance.

"There's bound to be a low or broken part
further down that we could just hope over".

Adam said he looked at Tom and Sarah
hoping they could add something.

"Yes but we need to pass through or we will
be stuck here and end up like them, for all
we know they may not be much to go back
to".

She said.

"No and stop blaming yourself again, you
could not have known this would happen,
how does this gate work can you overload
it".

Adam said.

"No but it take a Fair shaman to keep such a
large one open all the time, the one we
used was just a rift where the fabric of our
worlds is thin so with a little push and if you

know where to look, it is unstable so it may be possible".
"So we take out the shaman somehow".
Tom said taking them by surprise and all looked at him.
"Did I just volunteer myself".
He said it made them smile which he seemed to be able to do at just the right time.
"It could work but I just don't see away for us all to get out, it would be a great distraction which would give me time".
"Then we need to get him and the gate together".
Sarah said speaking for the first time.
"So this shaman what are we up against".
Adam said.
"It is a she, and like a Dryad can command and manipulate nature, so she will be corrupted and deadly".
Ithilli said.
With that said she pulled them back a ways then walked parallel to the wall and followed it for a while it was indeed in need of repair further down but still guarded they waited until it limped past there was no telling what gender if any it had they

moved in close then made a run for it and quickly managed to use its huge blocks as steps they hide among the rubble and debris of the other side well before been seen, they waited pulses racing, from their hiding place tents and makeshift buildings in row after row with thousands of the Wrong marching up and down.

"What are these stones you mentioned".

"There is a circle of them where the power is concentrated, like where we came through, even in your realm there are places of power, she will be there holding it open, which will take a lot out of her which is what we need".

Ithilli said.

"So we grab her and break her concentration, but we won't have much time".

Adam said.

"We should wait till it gets dark have a sneak round see where we need to be and what is about".

Tom said they agreed on this plan but they needed a better hiding place the three moved along and found a broken building with no roof but sides, so from there they waited till it grow dark and with that a coldness and a smog like fog settled in weather they could take advantage of the weather was another thing it did not give them much but at least hide them but at the same time they could not see much either. The four moved in as quietly as possible Ithilli leading the way, as they got close, Adam could not hear anything there was no talking or banter they just went on about their business the silence was unnerving, he realised these were no ordinary soldiers seeing them up close they were big he feared for the human race, how could they possible stand against them he did not know, there was a faint glow in the distance Ithilli nodded in that direction they moved on from the campsite and up the crumbling keep this gave them a place to hide and time to catch their breath.

"The shaman is there, when it glows the Wrong are passing through, we can't wait it's now or never".

Ithilli said but Adam was not so sure.

"Wait we can't just rush in, they will be onto us in moments, or just cut us down". Adam said.

"Let me distract them, I want to do this, you know there is no other way".
Tom said.
"You would be stuck here, we can't ask you to do this".
Ithilli said, but Tom did not give them chance he just ran and screamed and shouted at the top of his lunges the remaining three looked at each other than iIthilli set off to the glow, Adam looked back, the lad had balls he thought, and it worked, there were no guards here who would be here or attack surrounded like this just some three crazy enough, there were four tall pillar like stones which glowed as a continued line of the Wrong marched in and disappeared beside them stood the shaman it looked like she was growing out of the ground the earth seemed to pulse with power he could feel its pull throbbing in his chest and taking his breath away. It all happened so fast it was as if Ithilli went into a rage and ran at the shaman who seemed more tree and organic matter, Adam looked at Sarah the two did not know what to do, the Wrong did not seem to see or care and continued to march

in Adam pushed his way through taking Sarah with him heading for the light for an instant he saw Ithilli jump onto the figure and hacked and stabbed, the glow flickered and he knew it was now or never it was not until he grabbed Sarah's hand stepped through did he realised that Ithilli had scarified herself too, but it was too late.

*

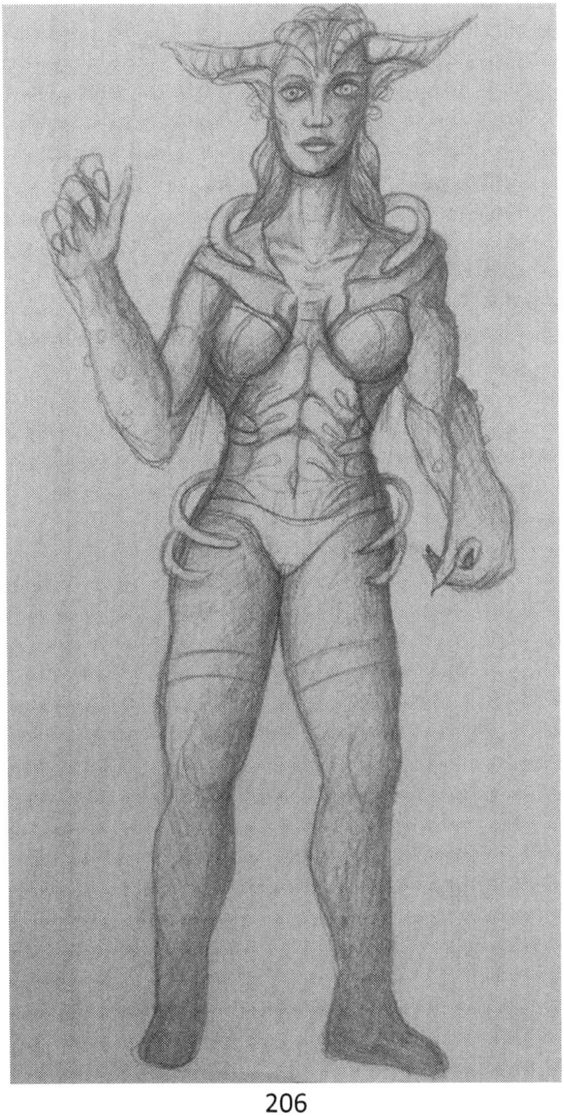

Marlitho Marlitho Thornbrook sat in front of her mirror looking at how perfect and beautiful she was with no shame, or care for what was going on and besides it was her doing and she smiled too it was all going to plan she had not counted on George causing so much trouble but the city would soon fall it was only a matter of time Ithilli had done her part even though she had no idea which made it all the more enjoyable for Marlitho. She finished getting ready to act all weak and afraid which was just not like her but then she was a good actor so it did not take long but just as she was about to leave her big full length mirror made a cracking sound she stepped back in front of it it had gone all dark with cracks all over it but when she saw herself and she did not like what was looking back she had clumps of her hair missing clothes all tatty and warn she was not her usual beautiful self but a hideous version long arms with claws horns and muscles she stepped back then the mirror changed to a dark cloud swirling round dark like a storm it formed a face that looked like death.

"Don't forget we put you where you are now and can soon take back the beauty that was bestowed upon you and your people".
It was the Ancients their voice spoke as if many voices were talking she felt it in her mind like a dark shadow pushing inside her right to her core she shivered.
"How could I forget O great ones".
She said and knelt down in front of the mirror.
"Our deal is close to completion Marlitho, don't let us down, you people have let the gift you were given go to waste instead you lay around in your decadence like you were at the top and like no other treating all those around you like dirt and seem to of forgotten who we rescued you from destruction. Soon we will all have what we want".
They said in a deep and booming evilness, which made her skin crawl and fear rise inside she had not forgotten their deal, the mirror cleared there were no cracks and she looked at her beautiful self again and sighed. They had once been creatures of ugliness fighting and killing each other beasts such as goblins, trolls and other

nightmare monsters then the first kind came the Ancients they offered them beauty to take all that was ugly away giving them greatness strong minds a future and in return on the day of the reckoning to reclaim what was given which was thousands of years ago now they were back the time seemed to of gone quickly Marlitho was ready but they had come a lot sooner her own plans were to keep what they had given and the Wrong will help her do this she wanted the Ancients power so they would kneel before her as would her own people and the weak humans and they would know fear but she would need all the pieces for this to happen it did not help that the humans kept getting in the way thinking they could stop this she just hoped Edward ludam will do his work and time to see what he is capable of she had seen a darkness inside him perfect for her needs even if she was just using him the humans were so easily manipulated and she love every second of it. There was a sharp knock at the door, she jumped a little bringing her back to reality, she opened it to find Rathan Stone and let out a sigh, he was like a love sick puppy following her around, it was sweet for a start but soon became tiresome.

"Are you okay, you look tired? I had to see if you were ok with what's going on".

He said.

"As you can see I'm fine, it was Ithilli with her sympathy for the humans, she must have released something when she stepped back into our world".

She said.

"What of George he has somehow seen the dark Ones among us, and trying to hunt them".

"I know you like these humans but he could cause us problems. And on top of this my sources have told me there is a new group in the city, some human cult, I need you to see into this, as for this breakout it could work to our advantage".

Marlitho said but Rathan did not look happy and gave her a puzzling look. She dismissed him.

*

They had kept Lucy locked in the room since the outbreak, the cult guard had given her water and a toilet break then tired her back to the chair, she managed a quick look out to see the streets were empty but for a few constables patrolling, a plan was already forming in her mind, they would all be distracted by what was going on, she did not want Matthew coming for her and falling into the Elect's trap. Lucy was curious and kept asking the guard what had happened, she was being nice to him, battering her eyelids, working her womanly charms on him, waiting for the right moment. He did not know much and was just a laky with muscles and not much else, which was perfect she thought.

The guard tired her back in the chair, but the knots were looser than before.
"You don't have to do this, my wrists are hurting, I don't want to go out there with those things roaming around".
Lucy said in her best weak girly voice, the man hesitated.

"Brother Longsfield told me not to trust you, and not to be tempted by you serpent charms".
She had to hold back a chuckle; it sounded almost word for word how the cult leader spoke.
"Where am I going to go, surely by now they must have locked the city down".
She said.
"You would get help from that Judas Matthew, and the supposed Father of Steam, now no more talking".
"Is Henry here, sorry Brother Henry".
She said to wind him up but also to gain information. Lucy wanted to do it that night, the big man mumbled about serpents again then left the room, she listened till his heavy foot fall were distant enough, having already loosed one of the chair legs, she gave the old dinners chair a quick wobble it it dropped free and the rest broke away dropping noisily to the floor one part had splintered leaving one part sticking up, she wriggled her hands free then grabbed a chair leg and stood ready for his return. Lucy called him back, she nearly went for the feeling sick trick but opted for good old

stand behind the door and hit him from behind. The Laky came, entering as he should and Lucy hit him with all she had but he just took the blow, she tried for a second but he blocked it and knocking it out of her hand, he grabbed her wrist.

"He was right, and I think you need to be taught a lesson, I won't damage that pretty face of your, but the rest I guess is mine he did not say anything about that".

He said and went for his belt, Lucy tried to pull free but her wrists were already too sore, he tried to kiss her and she stomped on his foot and tried to knee him in the crotch but hit his thigh instead.

"You are a feisty one, I like that".

He said touching her face then she bit his thumb, he screamed out then back handed her to the floor, she was dazed for a moment then the next minute he was trying to pin her down, pulling at her clothes then through tear filled eyes she saw the chair leg that was sharp, but it was just out of reach, then with all the strength she had left managed to grab it and buried it in his temple, he looked stunned and shocked then his body realised he should be dead, she was pinned by the very dead weight. It took her a few moment to wriggle free and straighten herself up then looked back at what she had done feeling ashamed and guilty, she pushed it to the back of her mind she had to escape.

Lucy left the room and entered the narrow corridor she knew one door was the toilet the second one she opened it a little and peered into the next room it was a kitchen, the disturbance and noise from their struggle had not brought anybody else, she entered and carefully left and peered out the back door, the backyard was small, a side gate took her Into an alleyway, she ran down it and burst out into the street and hit two constable they caught her.

"You have to take me to George now, it important".

She demanded, the two looked at her then each other confused but did as they were asked. Lucy walked between them along Corny street she could not believe how close they had been holding her, the two dropped her off at the Mayor's house now George's temporary headquarters, it was early evening and he was still there, he was surprised to see her having only seen her once.

"Get Matthew quick, I just escaped the Elect, they could be members among your staff".

She said he was confused but sent for the Preacher anyway he then sat her down and gave her water; her hands were shaking as she sipped it. Matthew burst in and ran to her.

"The leader Longsfield is here, and he wants you".

She said then told him the rest, he was not happy and there was still tension between him and George, but the big man still wanted to help.

"So how can we flush this cult leader out, or tell which among us are the sleepers".

He said to them both.

"I'm sure he will most likely know already, it will be a matter of time".

Matthew said.

"How will he retaliate".

George said.

"We need to keep going as normal, you will know him, he doesn't look like much, softly

spoken but with twin revolvers, which he can use, his members will have been split up with what happened, it won't be a frontal attack, we are all in danger here".
Matthew said.
"They are sick and fanatical, they see sin everywhere and in everyone they meet, his followers would die for him, their brains have been washed".
Lucy said.
"Yes it's hard to escape and get the man out of your head".
Matthew said.
"I don't like the idea of waiting for him to attack us".
George said.
"Then we call a meeting, rub their noses in it, call them names and how we will beat them, see who reacts, they don't like it and are very up tight".
Lucy said.
"Very well Matthew get onto it right away, we're having trouble containing those infected Fainters".
It was explained what had happened to Lucy, she was given a small back room that would have been servant rooms, not that

she cared, and with a freshen up and change of clothes it made her feel a little better, but sat waiting was the worst time she replayed the assault and escape, the vile man deserved it but it still made her feel bad having never taken a life. There was a gentle knock at the door, it was Matthew he was barely in when she embraced him and he held her back, then she broke down and cried it was like a flood gate opening, as if all that had happened to her all came out at once. He sat her down and held her hand, she kept apologising as she blurted it all out and he let her get it all out.

"I won't let him hurt you or your family again, he has to pay, these are my friends no harm will come to you here".

"It's not me I'm worried about, don't let him get to you, he has a way with words, he's the silver tongue devil".

"I won't fall for his words and lies this time Lucy, I was such a fool and I won't lose you again".

Then he gave her a gentle kiss and left, Lucy was a little shocked but liked it and smiled.

The meeting was called; big Richard was there, Matthew and George.

"Right then you lot, we are in a right bind here at the moment, with them Fainters trying to get in, but some Cult has moved in right under our very noses, they are operating right amongst us, we can't defend ourselves and our homes and families with enemies and those we can't trust".

He said in his usual booming Yorkshire accent, with no hairs and graces Lucy liked that about the man he was very charismatic too.

"I knew we cannot work with this shadow over us, we need teamwork not second guessing each other, and we need trust". Matthew said then it was Lucy's turn.

"They kidnapped me wanting to hold me to get to Matthew, they will stop at nothing, they murder and steal and say it in the name of The Lord of the spirits, saying it's justified".

Lucy said but nobody reacted just yet, but if they were among the survivors they would know they knew now.

"The man's name is Henry J Longsfield and he is their leader, he looks like anybody, a smooth talker but don't let that fool you, he will trick and play mind games with you. Do not trust this man, if you know anything or have any suspicions please don't hesitate or if you want to remain anonymous come to me, or a confession with me".

Matthew said and the meeting was done, they all went back to their posts and whatever the people were doing, the three went back to George's office.

"I guess we wait, but in the meantime Matthew I may have a problem to solve, in fact take Lucy and Richard as back up".

George said. Lucy was intrigued.

"This might sound stupid and unbelievable, we have a ghost problem".

He said.

"You're kidding right".

Lucy said.

"Yeah you won't believe what we have seen and done since the Fair Ones came, they brought with them all manner of creatures, end even a unicorn".

Richard said and she could see the big man was serious.

"Okay then lead on, seeing is believing I guess".

"That's the spirit pet".

George added and the three left, Matthew grabbed his bag and they were soon back to the empty streets.

"George has wanted to do this mission even before we sealed the city up, one you will be seen walking around with me and hopefully flush out H.J.L".

Matthew said as they came to a road called Goodramgate here the was an alleyway which the three entered, beyond this were many smaller back streets and houses with many turns.

"The restless spirits won't appear just yet, once it is close to dusk and the smog comes you will need this".

He pulled out a lamp its glass was tinted the same as the lens to spot the Dark Ones, he explained this to Lucy.

"You will see it with this light, it will appear hideous and will try to scare you and trick you".

"How do we fight a spirit, or get rid of it".

"Just let Mat do his thing while we watch his back".

Richard added putting an end to her questions.

The three sat on a low wall, it was chilly in the backstreet and the sun was low.
"So you two know each other". They nodded. "What's America like".
"Warmer and drier than here, I'm a reporter, my story the Fair Ones".
"You will have one hell of a story to tell after this".
He said, then the smog came but to Lucy it moved unnaturally, winding through the narrow streets, first at their feet then all around. Matthew stood up sudden and lit the lamp which he gave to Lucy she heard a whisper that made the hair on the back of her neck stand on end, Goosebumps crawled across her skin as it said her name in a woman's voice, the two men had not heard it though. *Do not believe all that is written, or what you are told, I can show you what is beyond your understanding. Come with us Lucy.* The whisper said inside her mind making her shiver. The smog swirled and figures made of mist surrounded them, Matthew looked worried, Lucy lifted the lamp and instantly regretted it, the figures began to change and rotten

flesh ripped and dropped their bony hands reaching out to her their rotting lips kept saying the same thing over and over in a moan. "Come with us, let us show you".
Lucy tried to pull back then Matthew spoke. "The Lord of the spirits on his throne of fire and light will see you judged, let that light touch you, although it is blinding don't be fearful, walk forward except this light, walk forward through the fire let its touch rise you up, let go of this world".

Matthew said the last part over and over, this made the spirits hesitate and shrink back, he raised his hand and his voice changed, growing deeper and more powerful, he spoke the words again and the spirits moaned losing their form, melting back and away then were gone, Lucy had never seen this side of him before, the power that came out of him could be felt in the air it was like something came over him. Another figure came out of the mist and smog but this was no ghost, it was a man with two revolvers which were pointing right at Matthew.

"Not seen a banishment like that for years, I knew you were special, so I have a one-time

offer, join us again brother, let us spread that light, and make them all see its power".
"Don't listen to him Matthew".
Lucy said. He put up a hand to silence her.
"I have seen that light already Longsfield. It is life, that sparks all around us, a new-born baby's first breath, and its first cry. Love that endures until our last breath, this is magical and powerful, you will never know of these things, you seek power, and a reward it will bury you Henry, you should be joining me".
"I will never join you Preacher".
And with that he pulled the triggers but Lucy had already seen this coming and she shoved Matthew out of the way and she took the two shots instead, Lucy dropped and Longsfield was gone Richard gave chase, Matthew held her.
"I'm cold Matthew".
"Don't speak Lucy my beloved, I see now what a fool I have been, the way I treated you, why o Lord why must you be taken from me".
He said holding her close.

"I love you Matthew King, with my last breath".
She said softly his words to Longsfield were so beautiful and moving she saw the hesitation in Henry, and that what was said rang true. Lucy saw the mist again but did not feel fear this time only a warmth, a familiar smell, a gentle word, his words echoed in her mind, she felt that magic touch her so deep and profoundly then of course that light.

Matthew King carried her dead body back, as he headed back Richard returned to his side.
"Sorry mate, I lost him, he won't get far I knew this city well".
"I want him alive, he will pay for his crimes, plus we can find the others of the Elect that are here, but there are other members around the world, it all started with him though, and I feel there is a connection with what is going on and the Fair Ones, Lucy stumbled onto something here too, we need to read her notes and what she might have learned".

Matthew said as they returned to George, they took care of Lucy's body using the police stations morgue, filled the man in on what happened and the cult leader was still at large.

Matthew went through her notes. The different people she had spoken too, even Ithilli who she mentioned the Book of Enoch to and it's similarities with Giants angels technology and secret knowledge, that and the Fair Ones. And an interview Rathan Stone one of the high Ones. It was Ithilli he wanted to speak too but she was still missing and of course Longsfield.

*

The two materialised and spilled out of a tear in the air and landed hard in the industrial sector, a scrap of rough land full of weeds between the buildings of the factors and workshops, Sarah had never felt so relieved to be back on earth with its smog and bad weather but she had twisted her ankle from the drop, but was happy to be back with its people's bad tempers and attitudes. Adam had made it through she had never felt so afraid when they had all been separated from each other in that horrible place the beasts how the place had felt like it was seeping into her soul she saw so much more than the others the Dryad and the Wrong were hideous and soulless things shallow husks she could see what was inside people the real person they were twisted and pure evil only speaking lies and half-truths only to cause chaos. Sarah followed Adam she felt she could trust him and the big man George they needed to get back to him and the city they had to be warned, they left and headed to the small city, Sarah limped but refused his help, she wanted to be stronger now, not wanting to be pampered and thought of as weak.

when they came across the main road, here there were humans but they seemed to be just standing around some just wondering about in an odd way, she stopped Adam going to them, something was not right here they were not normal she felt it, but it was too late one seemed to know they were there they turned and ran

after them with lifeless eyes, hands reaching out, they did not speak just an animal sound and were just as quick as them they had to run hard down the street but everywhere was deserted and boarded up the Wrong were nowhere to be seen not that it made it any less scary more were adding to the number behind and they did not seem to be tiring she was finding it hard to keep up with Adam but she did not want to show she was was just some weak girl but strong and a lot tougher and just wished she had kept herself in shape too much of her life been cooped up inside, hiding away from the crawl world not that running for her life was any better she had wasted too much time along and if she did die at least she had tried to do something about it and among friends, a figure dropped into the road ahead of them it was the one called the dweller an urban myth now very real she saw a confusion a duality inside him both a light and darkness she felt pity yet a loneliness like her own only wanting to belong, he ran to them.
"Quickly follow me and don't let them bite you".

He said which sounded a little odd to her but they did as he said and ran with them he took them from that street to and ally way which gave them a roof access and only just started climbing it before they were at the ladder the Dweller or Smity as Richard called him came up last and kicked those who were climbing giving the two time to get up and onto the roof, he then climbed up, turned and kicked the ladder dropping them off and hitting the ground hard the now three were safe for now Adam and Sarah were on their back gasping for air the Dweller left them for a moment then offered his hand to help them back up, Sarah took his warm smooth hand and felt his strength as she stood and for some reason felt giddy and gave him a hug which was just not like her and that felt good too she let go realising what she had just done and felt very awkward.

"What the hell just happen and why were we running from those crazy people".
Adam said.

"A lot has happened all will be explained when we reach George, for now follow me".

The dweller said Sarah looked over the wall there were a lot more people now and trying to reach them he took them across the rooftops she had to jump gaps that were very high but it was the perfect way to move about and escape they soon left the people who were after them behind and slowed a little, she then had chance to see what a forgotten world it was up so high and away from the trouble be low all most forgetting the views were breath-taking a different world that was above them the whole time too.

"So you see this every day? We are so taken up with life and never look up, what a wonderful place and safe too".

Sarah said as they took a breather and was very glad they did she had to remove the suit and felt a little ashamed of her sweaty under garments from wearing the suit for so long and running in it did not help either but the two did not seem to notice it as much as she did or they did not want to or too embraced and gentlemanly either way she was glad to be rid of it even though George had altered it but the thing was still

too heavy for her small frame and slim body size but it was a nice touch that he tried.
"One day I will take you to the minsters tallest part and you will see how truly great it is and that there is beauty here".
He said in his almost innocent way he too saw their world in a different way seeing beauty in things she took for granted it almost made her want to laugh and the want to hug him again came over her, she saw past his disfigured unhuman body and face corded muscles full of veins and strong it was then she realised she was staring at him again.
"We should get moving, we to have a lot to talk about with George".
Adam said breaking the awkward silence, the dweller nodded and they were off again Sarah had a spring in her step for a reason she did not quite know why but it got her clear across the city it was then that the Dweller stopped them right at the start of the boundary walls the roads in were blocked with a barricade of just about anything vehicles household junk crowds of the wandering people were gathering here and were been shot at the battlements had

a ragtag team of people defending it the bar walls too had they portcullises down the Dweller took them round showing the two what was happening.

"They are called the fainters they drop and die then come back to life and if you are bitten the same happens to you. And we don't know why or where it has come from".

He said pointing at more and more gathering they just grunted and clawed at the walls and barricades trying to get in, Sarah shivered and not from the cool evening air he then took them to a building that was close to the walls he had a plank of wood ready so they could walk across to safety Adam went first and easily made it with only a few wobbles, it did not look that far but when Sarah stood upon it and the first thing she did was look down, the Fainters below had sensed she was there and it was sending them into a frenzy this only made things worse it now looked even further, she took one step then wobbled then climbed back down.

"It's ok Sarah just listen to my voice I'll walk you through it, keep looking forwards, blank out what is going on around you".
She did as he said and was almost across when a gunshot went off in the distance she wobbled and fell she grabbed the board but her legs were dangerously close the Fainters grabbing hands she screamed and the board shifted she saw them reaching for her with their dead blank eyes she couldn't hold on much longer she dropped but her whole world just turned upside down one second she was falling the next it felt like she was flying through the air held in a tight grip then she felt cold hard stone of the battlement beneath her stood over her was the dweller and she knew right away he had rescued her, he helped her up but she was still a little shaken up and grazed her pulse racing and not all because of the incident, the board had been lost and too close for her comfort she looked back out now felling a tiny bit safer it help he was stood next to her out there were hundreds all heading their way. They were then taken to see George here the Dweller left them much to her disappointment.

*

George looked tired and gaunt stood in a large office of the fair building.
"And about bloody time, where's Ithilli".
He boomed at the two
"Hello to you to and were just fine by the way".
Adam said sarcastically, the big man was not giving them a warm welcome and was not his usual joyful self a very changed man a shadow of his former self, he told the big man about what had happened to them in the Fair realm and that they had lost her and Tom. George did not look any happier on hearing this news, then it was his turn to tell him what was going on, it had been two months when to Adam it had only been about three days.
"I lost Jillith to those bastards I had to take her life or she would of comeback as one of them, and they just keep coming even in here despite how self-contained we are and the work it took, we keep finding them".
George said Adam could now see why he was so sad and biter so he regretted been

so sarcastic. George described what had happened with her and the city but no clue to how or who was the first to pass it on.
"Oh and that's not all there have been other fatalities we have found people as if frozen by fear".
It sounded like his first investigation he told George what he had seen and tried to find out about and the Justice of the peace had warned him off and sacked him.
"The Dark Fair Ones are not capable of this or the fainters there's more going on here, the City is yours find out what you can come and meet the team".
He said then led Adam and Sarah out into the city's square Richard was there and a lot more too, stood beside them was a new one called Edward, George had been very busy more suits and the huge amazing Walkermotive with huge guns walking trains of armour and steam, even Fair ones stood among them they were willing to help now as they too were in danger, George introduced him to them and to give him anything he might need in his investigation and not to hold anything back because they were all to work together and they listened

to him the big man had already gone through enough but he was confident now, stronger. Adam wanted to help him as much as he could he sent them all back to their posts.

"We have guards day and night Walkermotives at the main gates and bars, patrols, the constables might listen to you more than me, I don't know how long we can hold out, ammo is low and so will be our food".

He said, the constables seemed like a good place to start but it was getting dark and so said good night to him and Sarah she went with him as Adam went back to his old Flat it was cold and dark so he lit a few candles and the fire took off his armour and clothes then dropped onto the bed having never felt so tired and glad of a warm bed.

Chapter 7

The dweller followed them across the rooftops but his thoughts were elsewhere it was Sarah; it was the way she looked at him without fear, pity or judgment but who he was as if seeing right inside him, she brought out old feelings that rose in him stirrings and emotions long forgotten, her warm touch and felt lost in her blue eyes, pulse racing, a smile on his lips that softened the frown on his face was it possible she had feelings for him, he looked down at his body then was hit by another flashback his hands were smoother with no claws but they were covered in blood he wore fine armour bodies lay at his feet a sword of shining steel dripping with gore, hear the moans of death from both sides, he shook his head and was back on the rooftops it kept happening more and more, like old repressed memories were fighting to be free and were becoming even more intense and stayed with him but it was still just bits and pieces. He watched them leave and made for his bell tower, he could still smell Sarah's sent on him which made him think of her again and a warm feeling in his loins he fell asleep with a smile such a thing was alien to his lips.

*

Adam woke early the next day but did not feel any better for the sleep his body still ached he headed for his old office the streets were empty now, the law was gone they had no power over now, the government was gone and the law with it the sergeant was gone only a few constables remained but on seeing him they were very willing to help and said the thought it was bad they sacked him in fact they treated him a whole lot better so he took them to have a meeting to see George once there they looked at a map of the city put pins in where the incidents had occurred for the fainters and the murders, Adam sent out constables to find any witnesses and to see if they could find anything. But he needed more help and knew the Dweller would have seen more from the rooftops then most having tried to reach him before all this started as a witness and decided to take Sarah too and the two had something going on between them which was quite cute their lives had been so isolated and lonely they seemed so innocent and made for each other so she was sent for, Adam headed to the minster the streets were empty with a strange silence no hustle and bustle of workers, sight seers and markets just litter blowing about, armed people here and there he called out and did not have long to wait before he dropped down silently behind him but Adam knew he would be there the two headed back to George.

"I was looking for you before this happened and was hoping you might have witnessed something back then and now".
Adam said.
"Somebody is letting them in right under our noses at night, I've walked the walls it is very secure, the fainters are mindless and could not just make their way in".
He said.
"So about the murders, where their very life seems to have been sucked out of them, what could be doing this, a Fair one maybe".
"No its something else doing this".
They reached George's office and the Dweller told them what he knew and that somebody is working on the inside one of the elder Fair Ones came in to try and help which they now seemed more willing to do and maybe the fact they were not immune to the Fainters bite, she looked old and hunched over the once red hair was now all but white, she glanced at the Dweller for a moment frowned then back at Adam who described the other victims.
"You have a Succubus problem".

The Elder Fair one said as a matter of fact like it was something that happened all the time.

"So how do we hunt such a thing".
Adam said.

"It will have a layer close by where the victims were found she won't wonder too far, midnight is when she will make an appearance, baiting her will help old or young small very opportunistic, but this one sounds quiet forward and confidant, oh they can be strong if cornered and will try and deceive and tempt you".

She said and looked at Sarah and the others did the same even without words she know what they wanted her for, Sarah was small and be perfect bait.

"No! It's too dangerous".

The dweller said making it obvious he liked her and she blushed.

"I can look after myself you know, I'll do it".
Sarah said, it was directed at him and everybody else they could see she was not to be messed with and was very feisty and none were about to argue, they asked the Elder Fair One about the fainters and that some body was letting them in.

"I don't see why it would be one of my people or what there was to gain, I will ask around I know many still don't like humans but we have no choice now we have to work together".

And with that the meeting was over, Adam felt she was holding more back, then the old elder took him to one side.

"Ithilli is my daughter and you must be the mortal she has feelings for, I feel her she still lives".

She said surprising him but she was already living the room and gone.

He then joined the others and grabbed food sitting in the old mayor's home it was very elegant and posh but for most of them they would ever see in their lifetime. Adam was sat with Sarah and the Dweller.

"Have you ever come across a Succubus Smity".

He asked the Dweller.

"I remember very little from my past, there are many creatures of myth from the dark realm that have come through or were brought here, they may of slipped through".

He said not really liking his nickname but he could not remember his own name let

along his past so it would have to do for now, it was midday and they had some hours to wait till midnight before they needed to get ready to hunt the succubus and so decided to meet later so Adam left the two alone he wanted to talk with the Elder again but just him and her so he had a look around and found her in the back it was a little garden area out the back hidden from view, she did not look surprised to see him the Fair Ones could not use their charm on him it just gave him an headache when they tried and visiting their realm had hurt his head, she was sat on a bench there were potted plants and hanging baskets and it smelt nice, a secret garden away from it all.
"I come here to think sometimes, I feel we brought help to you humans but our own problems to, our past is a very colourful one, I see that the wool can't be pulled over your eyes".
She said.
"We need full disclosure, we've all done things were not happy with, but if there is anything your holding back or have that we should know now is the time, your charms don't work on me".

Adam said, and she smiled
"We have suspected one of our own and responsible for the recent events, we have a long history and guilt of the things we have done, I see no reason to hide it from you now and couldn't anyway, and we are just as much in danger now as you".
She said and Adam sat next to her.
"There is a legend that a Fair One that will return and he will have to choose between who shall rise or fall good or bad, he changed our people seeing how bad we had become, he stood up for the less beautiful and less fortunate the underdog, and raised an army, even though he lost it made my people think about what they were turning into so instead of killing him he was spared, and exiled taking the forgotten a mind cleansing so to speak".
She said and Adam was still trying to take it all in, he let her continue.
"The complexity doesn't stop there or our story, the Dark Dryad you spoke of he was called Luthano Rockheart, but she broke that heart of stone, but one other also loved him but he did not feel the same thus

she became bitter, I suspect I know who she is but have no proof".
She said.
"And I think I knew where he is, the Dweller, he has no memory of his past and he has the look of a Fair one, this can't be a coincidence".
Adam said.
"Yes I suspect you are right, I must speak with him again, but for now back to our history, we were responsible for the human race but from where we come from goes back a long way, The Ancients the First Ones only they could be responsible for the Fainters and the Wrong only they have power, this could only mean their return and the one here has let them through or done some kind of deal".
She said and it was a lot for him to take in, she sent for the Dweller to come to her, Adam could see why all this was kept so quiet the church would not want such knowledge out the bible was everything and god's hand was everywhere, living a life full of morels and god fearing so if this got out it would make things worse if that was possible they already blamed the Fair Ones

for the decline of their numbers attending the church and industrialization and urbanization, so there has always been tension but on the other hand the Fair Ones had helped so much putting England on the map, they spoke more while waiting.

"So there could be more creatures like the Succubus".

He asked.

"What I think is happening, and coming are the Ancients, if they enter the human realm escaping the Hollow beneath the earth it will bring the end, Ragnaroc, apocalypse and the end of days it has many names".

She said. George had mentioned the Hollow Earth theory and would have to be told about all of this.

"But how can we hope to stop such a thing from happening".

"The one I spoke of the Chooser I suppose". She said and the Dweller entered with Sarah, the Elder looked at him up and down then reached a hand out he was confused as she touched him they both feel back as if a shock had just hit them.

"It is he; I just broke the spell of the forgotten".

She said shaking her hand and flexing it the Dweller or Luthano Rockheart was very confused as was Sarah.

"Once he remembers then we will have the one responsible among us but I don't know what else it will bring, because the spell affected my people too so he too was wiped from our memories as we were from his".

She said. Luthano Rockheart had to sit down and did not look well holding his head and Sarah was not happy at what her beloved was now going through and she glared at the Elder and Adam, Luthano got up and stormed out leaving them all looking at each other Adam tried to explain it to Sarah but she was not happy and went after him he let her go.

"Give him time it will be hard and may come to him in bits and pieces".

The Elder said Adam thanked her and he too followed them.

Chapter 8

The dweller walked away his mind confusion he needed space to think he jumped up to his world ran and jumped trying to make sense of the flood gates that had just opened up in his mind, images thoughts and feelings all hitting him all at once and felt like his head was about to explode he climbed to the highest tower and looked over the city and beyond his brooding place and right then he did have a lot to think about, his feeling for Sarah were mixed in with the confusion but one name did stick out, Marlitho then he remember the battle the war he had caused between them, and the Dryad that had tricked him the history of the Fair Ones and those that had died because of him, guilt washed over him like a cold wave the dream of blood on his hands had been right how could he have been so blind and stupid, Marlitho had caused it all they had forced him to take the forgotten and be exiled, but now he remembered and they were going to pay big and this time he would not need an army just his hands around Marlitho's throat now they had spread their sickness to the humans blinding them to, but for Adam and George and of course Sarah who despite regaining his memories still had feelings for her and that there was hope for the humans yet yes they were floored and weak bodies and minds but even when face by incredible odds kept on fighting, a spirit his own people did not possess.

It was getting dark and he would have to face his friends again try and not scare them because of the coming darkness he knew they would fight to the end till every

last one fell but not be broken he admired them for that and their loyalty it would be a great honour to fight beside them, it almost made him laugh that the humans hated each other were selfish and stubborn but in the end they would sacrifice themselves and died for their fellow man these were a people he would fight for and were worth it having watched over them for so long even now surrounded by so much death could still laugh and joke with each other it was denial but it was their coping method and they still got on with it he felt proud of them too his first port of call wanting to apologise for running away it had been a moment of weakness not something that was about to happen again or any time soon he found her on the wall, walking by herself he made sure she saw him not wanting to frighten her with his silent approach he walked beside her for a moment.
"I'm sorry Sarah for shutting you out like that I had to try and clear my head, I remember everything, and we are all in danger, and some of it my doing".

He said and she gave him more silence and just as he thought she was ignoring him she broke her silence.

"If we are to be together Luthano then there should not be anything that we can't get through no lies just pure honesty I could see it hit you hard, and if you need time".

She said and he took her hand and pulled her in close to him.

"I will do as you ask Sarah nothing will be kept from you, you see the world so different you are stronger than you think you are, and I want you in my life".

He said and before she could speak he kissed her gently at first till their passion grew and she did not pull away helpless in his arms and weak at the knees the whole of her body felt like nothing else and her sent aroused him they broke apart looked into each other's eyes nothing was said and they kissed again his pulse raced, but this was not the time or place.

"I will tell you everything about me now and not just the bad I want to show you so much wonder and beauty to take you away from all of this pain and misery you will never have to be lonely again just because you are different I've been that way all my life too, I tried to change those around me and it cost me everything".

Tears had welled in his eyes has he spoke every word was like a weight lifted it was like she understood him having suffered herself at the hands of her own like he had and it was wrong, she touched his cheek wetting her fingers as she wiped away the tears of his pain then licked her fingers it was the most erotic thing he had ever seen it made him smile almost hearing his own pulse and was not the only thing throbbing. A guard walked past the two they had been so lost in each other has he said good evening this broke their spell bringing them back to reality.

"Right we have a Succubus to take care of let's find Adam".

Luthano said and he liked it when she said his name there had been a void now it was full of love, Sarah had to compose herself.

"Yes my lover, let's have one less thing hunting us".

And he had to agree.

*

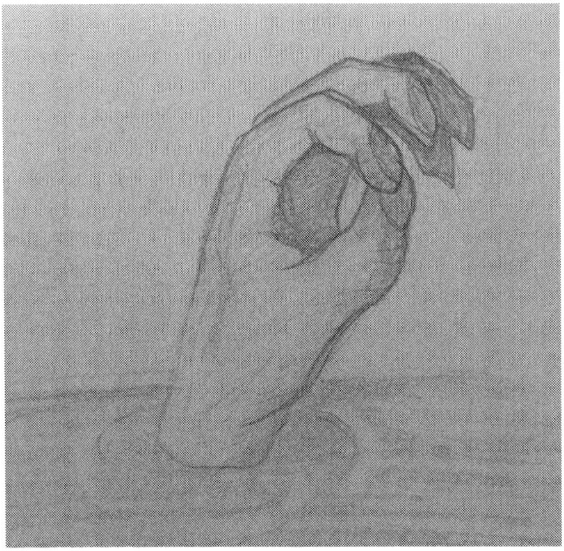

Adam had been telling George about what he had learned from the Elder and more things were coming and it was far from over when Luthano and Sarah entered and were very cosy with each other but it was nice to see he looked like a changed man walking with his head up a confident stride even a hint of a smile the lines of his face smoother.
"We still have a job to do".
Luthano said Adam looked at the time it was only a few hours till their hunt would begin.
"What will we need to kill it and anything we should know".
Adam said.
"Removing the head is the way to go, they can be tough and have long claws that can cause damage and infection too, so stay back".
Luthano said.
"What's the plan".
Sarah said.
"You need to be careful and act lost and weak, we will do the rest, don't' underestimate it".
Luthano said to her and Adam.

"And good luck to you, when you are back there is much to speak about".
George said. And with that they headed out to the dock area the two main bridges were barricaded the Fainters were gathered there at the water's edge but were just stood about and it was now dark they seemed dormant, the three move as quiet as possible to the area Adam had found the body and the others had been in the same place close to the gatehouse where the section of the Skeldergate bridge that could be lifted for the bigger boats to enter the dock. Sarah sat on the wall while Adam and Luthano hide close by behind the trees that ran along the river Ouse it was muddy where the river had rose high and reseeded making it slippery under foot. It had gone midnight there was a low mist on the water and all was quiet they were getting cold and restless Sarah move down closer to the water's edge then from within the dark shadows beneath the bridge long strong white pale arms reached out without a sound and grabbed Sarah one hand over her mouth the other round her waist and pulled her up among the metal dirt and

cobwebs she did not have time to scream and couldn't move pinned down by a hideous hag with wrinkled skin and sagging breasts but despite how old she looked she was very strong Sarah tried to struggle to pull away from her pale lined face and bad breath gapped teeth that were black and rotten.

"You're a feisty one aren't you, you will taste so much sweeter oh and innocent blood too ummm".

She said smacking her wet lips together and licked black dribble away. Adam lost sight of Sarah, he grabbing a torch. Luthano ran to the water's edge and saw footprints in the mud fearing she had fallen into the cold dark dangerous water that had already claimed so many lives, he called out to her softly Adam searched and called too Luthano cursed himself for missing her then the two heard a muffled sound a scream from under a hand coming from the bridge, they ran slipping and sliding but still could not see her, then another scream and a splash it was Sarah hitting the water, Adam dived in while Luthano faced the Succubus she was very tall with a long reach.

"The forgotten one, you will pay for costing me my pray".
She said and spat at him Luthano pulled out his sword.
"What do you know of me?"
He said as they circled each other.
"The vale has dropped non are safe now, the Ancients and all who hate you knew where you are now, ha ha ha you have damned yourself".
She said mocking him, he slashed at her but she was very fast but he did not want her dead too quickly.
"Tell me what you know and I will make it a quick death".
He said.
"Such sweet talk Luthano, there are so many more horrors to come, more than you could handle".
She said and a single shot stopped her and she shuddered and her chest exploded covering Luthano in her black thick blood.
"Good because he won't be on his own".
Adam said as she dropped to the ground blood coming out of her mouth Luthano put his blade to her throat but she was laughing at them so he cut her head clean off with

one single swipe picked it up and throw it in the river along with the body, he turned to Adam a very wet Sarah was leaning on him and did not look happy at all.
"Where the hell were you two, having a bro-mance or something?"
She said as they headed back. They got back and Sarah went to get cleaned up the two sat in the lounge still to hyper from the kill to sleep.
"There's a lot you need to tell us, I heard it the elder spoke of the Ancients too".
Adam said tea was brought for them.
"They have lain dormant for centuries they are the creators of all things, creatures of nightmares too, they live deep beneath the earth in the Hollow".
He said and took a sip Sarah rapped in a thick night gown joined them.
"Did it hurt you, the scratch is deadly".
"I'm fine Luthano my so called protector".
But she was being sarcastic.
"Let me rest and try to gather my thoughts and meet with George in the morning, it is too late now".
He said and they had to agree so went back to their rooms Sarah stayed back with

Luthano she kissed him and smelt very nice to him he returned the kiss but pulled away.
"Don't take this to heart but my head is boiling over at the moment give me time Sarah my beloved".
He said softly she nodded and gave him a warm smile.
"I'm a Fair One and I love you but I will also out live you, you will age as I cannot, I'm sorry but maybe we should rethink this".
"No, Luthano don't speak like that, we could still find a way to be together".
"Maybe when this is over but it could be the end of the world".
"Then all the good reason when we both might not have much time left".
She said and had a good point he held her hand and kissed her on the forehead they went to separate rooms.

*

Marlitho stood in front of Edward as he told her what he had learned but she had felt the Vale drop.
"Luthano is the Dweller and he remembers all but is still confused, oh and he loves a

woman called Sarah some lady or baroness, Adam the constable as returned too, but no Ithilli".

He said.

"Good you have done well, now let more of the Fainters in".

He nodded and left he was starting to irritate her now but had brought great news and results, she smiled that her beloved had returned but the woman was human so the two could not be together this made her smile even more it was perfect she would make great leverage, Marlitho decided to wait for him to come to her she was still shaken by the Ancients visit and what their plans could be, the rising of the dead and creatures, all signs pointed to them bring about the end of days but why, she did not have all the answers it was then a seed of doubt dropped they were not noted has been trustworthy they had promised her a place at their side, she still had work to do, George would have to go he continued to amaze her and she did admire his tenacity and the other humans they were not that easy to break as she had first thought but all the better she did not want to reveal herself just yet, the timing had to be right but she could not wait to see Luthano's face when he sees her and make him hers so they could be as one like it was supposed to be and was written, he would learn to love her in time or those he loved would suffer as would all of the humans she would be taken seriously once and for all they would bend a knee and so would the rest of their world.

*

Once word got out about Luthano's return all the Fair Ones came to see him, they chanted his name even the Elder Ones came, when once he had thought himself a freak a monster that made people run in fear from him or just the mere mention or a half breed then on top of that found love in a beautiful woman who was extraordinary and strong minded but now having his memory back was a two edged blade it was great having his past back but he was almost immortal now and she was not her life time would past in the blink of an eye to him she would grow old and die he could not face it but he could not just turn away from her, to Sarah it did not matter but to him it hurt like hell, they had made love and he knew it was a mistake but it had felt so nice to have her so close he remembered the long cold nights in the bell tower then from that to holding her so close. He stood before them all they wanted him as their leader but there was one he was looking for and that was Marlitho but her face was not among them but they had seen her which only made her all the more guilty and responsible and so told them she was a suspect and if seen should be brought before him, Luthano was curious to see her though, to ask her why he remember the trial when they brought him before the very ones he stood in front of now when they ran his sentence for treason made him responsible for the deaths so they had to vote for either the death sentence or taking the Forgotten and be exiled she had voted for the latter as had most but somehow they took pity for him he was not tall and handsome like them or smartly dressed he hated them for that but also regretted it the

deaths had not made him feel any better
and felt guilty and would of taken death
over the hell he was living through now it
was as if he was still been punished when
all he had wanted was to do good, make
them equal, make them see how bad they
had become and now they wanted him
because they were afraid so it was only pity
he felt now and as for the humans they had
more than proved themselves and of course
Sarah his beloved he would hold hell off for
her and it was like it was about to happen
there was going to be a time for choosing a
test and right now it was the humans he
would have on his side and at his back yes
they had their flaws but so did his people
and had gone through their very own dark
times and the very few Fair ones had
wanted to help them, he did decide to lead
them at least he would know what they
were up to instead of Marlitho, he called
and end to the meeting he needed to speak
with George he had a theory it was then he
heard breaking glass which seemed very
odd they all went to see, outside there
were hundreds of birds mostly crows, they
were swarming and just throwing

themselves at the windows and attacking people some screamed others panicked he had seen this before and knew what was to follow other creatures of night terrors this was the sign of the harpies creatures of myth to the humans but very real to him, first the succubus and more were to follow so he rushed over to George and grabbed Adam, Sarah and Richard over to the big man's office.

"I heard you speak of the Hollow Earth theory, it's true by the way".

He let that sink in before continuing.

"There is a hole close by here in England that's where these things are coming from and more will be heading this way take a zeppelin and blast it we need to slow these attacks down before we are overwhelmed".
Luthano said.

"So I guess you're in charge now".
George said.

"Yes they now all look to me, but it was not always this way they were the ones who exiled me, but who else would you have, you know I want the same as you in this, and they will listen to me".
Luthano said.

"It sounds good to me, I trust him, and if he is right we might not last much longer".
Adam said, George reluctantly agreed, Luthano did not want to stand on his toes or take away his leadership.
"Very well, I just hope you are right and this doesn't just piss them off even more".
He said.
"Yeah but we have a problem we won't reach the Zeppelin let alone fly it".
Sarah said referring to the birds.
"Harpies will be our next task after the succubus".
The humans knew about this one more than the other.
"So how will we tackle these things and the birds".
"They don't have any abilities and are more of a nuisances, but they can be deadly too, what I suggest is that we go at night they won't fly in the dark, as for killing them, shoot them out of the sky and find their aviary before they get too comfortable".
Luthano said.
"So about this hole and entrance to Hollow Earth, do you know the size and what will be needed explosive wise".

"Well all I know is that it's in Staffordshire and at the two poles the north and south of your world, there may be others".
Luthano said.
"I have done my research and will have another look into this other hole".
George said and was very excited about it.
"I guess we're on bird and beast duty".
Adam Watts said.
"Yes that is a great idea, take a team, ware your suits, use flames Harpies hate fire".
With that the meeting was at an end Luthano watched them all leave. If the Ancients were in deed coming then there was to be hard times ahead he thought and just hoped they were strong enough, Sarah came over to him and when the room was empty they embraced but she could see he was troubled and always made him feel stronger even without speaking he kissed her forehead.
"You have the weight of the world on your shoulders; don't keep it all to yourself".
Sarah said he sighed knowing she was right having gone from nothing and now the leader all over again his mind was still a mass of confusion more and more came to

him each day, some without warning
flashes and half thoughts it was frustrating
for him but one thing that did remain true
was his feeling for Sarah there were no
confusion there, she was his link to reality a
rock, his lighthouse in the fog of his mind, a
guide home.

*

Adam watts suited up he was teamed up
with Richard and two other men he had not
worked with before but George had given
them to him so he supposed he would not
of given them if they were no good, they
grabbed weapons shields and stepped
outside. The sound came first, a cacophony
of bird calls and crowing in the thousands it
was not a nice sound more like fingernails
on a chalkboard, the swarm came at them
hard it was difficult to see as the crows
came in hard and they were not small in
size either they had to link their shields
together Roman soldier style, a
Walkermotive was called in with a
flamethrower while those on foot used
shotguns and blunderbuss but they did not

seem to do any good there was just far too many, the big walking train helped as it belched out flames the birds did not like it. Adam had to pull the men back, the birds just kept dive bombing them even with the armour it hurt peeking at their eyes causing confusion, then as quick as they came the swarm of birds were gone a big shadow passed over head they looked up to see a humanoid figure with wings were arms should be it had short legs with big bird like talons where feet should be and looked very dirty, the Harpy swooped in low and back up into the sky as it was met by flames and let out a half scream half squawk it was fast Adam felt the up draft from its powerful wings , it avoided their shotguns and flames staying just out of reach having used the birds as a gauge testing them first Adam guessed he decided to pull them back as another Harpy joined it throw a huge stone at them with its talon feet it hit a shield denting it but none were hurt, they made their way back to the mayor's house running along High Peter gate and Stone Gate more stones rained down on them the Walkermotive was dented they needed another plan but it was getting dark while they were away boards had been put up against the windows that had been broken by the birds. The Dweller/Luthano met them once inside.

"Now that is dusk we should take a small team, I will take to the high ground and rooftops, we must stop them otherwise they will not let us reach the airship".

Luthano said and they took this to George who was more than willing for them to do this, and told them to take Edward and Richard. The four went out onto Blake Street, Luthano disappeared quickly scaling the walls they headed down Davygate, it was all quiet and eerie there were dead birds on the pavement.

"So you actually went to another world where the Fair uns came from, what was it like".

Edward said.

"It was not great, I wouldn't recommend it".

Adam said.

"Wattsy here would go anywhere if Ithilli were there".

Richard said.

"So he likes a Fair un, don't they live like forever or something".
Edward said he too had a broad accent.
"Okay you two shut up".
Adam said just as Luthano appeared.
"They've taken up residence at Monkgate Bar on the battlements".
They ran over to Goodramgate but stayed back peering out from the alley just down from the blocked Bar. Then pulled back they needed a plan.
"Guess you tackled these too, anything we need to know".
Adam asked.
"Don't underestimate them they are strong especially their legs. Two of us will come at them on the walls while two will distract from the ground, I counted three".
Luthano said but they still had to decide who would do what, of course Luthano would go up top and he picked Edward to go with him so Adam and Richard would stay down. They waited while the other two got into position, then moved in talking loudly on purpose and marching around causing as much noise as possible and it did the trick the Harpies hated it and started

squawking and complaining, Richard brought out his massive Blunderbuss and loaded it, Adam had his hand cannon ready, Luthano and Edward attacked, one flew up the other down and was met by buckshot to the face and dropped to the pavement in a cloud of black dirty feathers, the third swooped down at Adam clawed feet first and knocked him down and the wind out of him, ripping and scratching at his chest plate, he tried to fight it off but it was too strong, something heavy knocked the beast of it was Richard having kicked it, Adam was up wasting no time and shot it with his weapon right in the face which was human yet had a beak and the torso had small human female breasts, it was a strange creature up close. There was one left which tried to take off but Luthano jumped up catching its legs his weight pulled it back down and the two disappeared behind the battlements they did not see him finish it but seeing black blood over him was a good sign that the Job was done.

The four returned to George on the way back Adam spoke with Luthano.

"There's a lot that has been bugging me of lately, be straight with us, what else have you Fair Ones not being telling us".
"You have a quick mind and I can see not much can get past you".
"It's not that us humans aren't grateful, but there is always a price, what do you want in return".
Adam said.
"We are losing our home, you have seen our realm, we have brought it on ourselves, I know that we are no better, always fighting amongst ourselves".
"So you give us some knowledge to ease your guilt then slowly take over".
"That's one way to put it, but that's not going to happen now that I'm here".
"That's good to hear, I'm glad you're here, what else should we expect from them".
"We must remain vigilant, that and the mole that is among you".
Luthano said.
"Well that is at the top of my to do list, I have my constabulary on patrol out there".
George had gone to bed so they did the same, Adam returned to his flat it felt like forever since he had left, it was cold and

empty with just the mattress on the steel bed frame, he stripped off the armour and dropped onto it and fell asleep missing Ithilli.

Adam Watts returned to the Mayor's house, the others were there and they filled George in on what had happened but he was ill and not himself, quick to anger and told them to get out. It was then Luthano called Adam over and spoke so only he could hear him.
"I've seen this mood change before, he might have a Hex or curse on him, this could be another attack, we must do our investigation there will be signs, but keep this between us two for now".
"So what do you think it could be".
Adam asked.
"A Hag or witch as you might know them".
"Where would such a thing hide in York, and what signs do you mean".
"Milk and food going sour, animals acting strange, miscarriages the list is big depending on what type".
"Well things can't get any stranger round here".

Adam said and Luthano had to agree.

*

Edward slipped away to meet with the Fair One female and he hated the way she treated him and ordered him around, he had being promised so much and was starting to regret his new employment. They always met in different places; he filled her in on what was going on and told her it was getting hard to keep letting in the fainters in with the constables everywhere. "George has to go and as for Adam he is starting to be a royal pain too, now go and do as I ask, time is running short".
"You are asking too much of me they have already suspected there is a mole, it's too risky".
Edward said trying to stand up to her.
"I'm sure I can find another, are you having second thoughts Ludlam, you would regret ever crossing me, now get out of my sight". She said and her yellow and orange eyes seemed to glow and he felt his head spinning, Edward pulled back in fear his pulse racing, the feeling passed as he

moved away and resigned to the fact he was stuck with her, the thing was he was not wanting to leave because of George and the others or was wrong having only done this for himself and felt no guilt, they had done nothing for him he had worked in the hot weaving factory, long hours and low pay, the same everyday day in day out with only Sunday off, if they were lucky, with no overtime pay, it was mind numbing. It had been exciting hunting down the Harpies, being part of a team and from the strange things he had seen, Edward know she had some kind of hold over him. He made his way back so he was not missed a middle aged man approached him as he was heading back.

"Can you help me young man, I'm afraid and have been in hiding I may be able to help somehow".

"Yeah sure, we need all the help".

Edward said and took him back to the headquarters, George was not seeing anyone so more places were set up, he gave the man some food and measured up for a suit.

*

Matthew King and Richard had been searching the city for Longsfield but had come up empty handed; it was frustrating and angered him. With the Harpies and everything else going on, the man was slippery.

"Maybe the birds got him, or the Succubus".

Richard said Matthew knew the big man was only trying to help.

"No he's a very resourceful man, let's get back".

The two returned to the mayor's house but a temporary office had been set up so they did not have to keep bothering him, he had a lot of pressure on him, from inventor to leader had taken its toll on him. Longsfield had prayed on him it's what the man did, Matthew had lost his faith having lost all who were close to him at his lowest point the man had come to him shown him the road back to his salvation and had restored his faith in the Lord of the spirits, they all followed him like he was some Holy spiritual leader, a messiah and they would do anything for him, even persuaded him to make friends with Lucy and her father, he fell in love with her and she made him see the real world again and he was been manipulated he tried to leave the Elect and the man's hold over him, this caused conflict inside him, confusion and inner turmoil. He escaped to England worked as a Preacher made friends and met George but even England was not far enough to escape the Elect.

*

Adam followed Luthano around the city taking him to places and alleyways he did not know even existed.
"I know that the Fair One charm or Vale doesn't work on you, the Hag will be using it either to hide her appearance or her lair. Do you feel sick or your pulse race like when you are around us".
"Yes and headaches too".
"Good use it, tell me if you feel anything as we walk round".
Luthano said and they headed over to the riverside and his old beat, it was on the

dock at the crane tower where he felt sick, there had been no work there everything was dropped and abandoned he nodded at Luthano but he kept on walking passed then stopped further up.

"We will come back tonight we have a lot to prepare for and we might need back up".

Luthano said and the two returned to Georges new headquarters, but as they got there two guards stood at the door and stepped in front when Adam approached.

"We're here to see George, it's me Adam Watts".

"Sorry but Mr Stephenson is otherwise engaged and doesn't want to be disturb". The guard said.

"I'm Luthano I'm the leader of the Fair Ones, you can't refuse me entry".

"Those are his orders".

"He's not himself, surely you can see that, he's clearly not thinking straight, now tell him who's here".

Adam insisted but the guard stood his ground as did the second one, they put a hand to their sidearms, Luthano pulled Adam away.

"Not here friend, he is into the paranoid stage, we must end it tonight, we can't lose him, he is the symbol of strength whoever it is doing this they know what they are doing, we stop the Hag and then find out who is behind this".

"I don't have my armour or our weapons".

"Come with me I have a cache of weapons and what we'll need".

Luthano said and they headed over to the Minster, Luthano climbed up the east side of the massive building and was gone, two minutes later he returned with a bag and opened it not even out of breath, inside were a sawn off shotgun, a large revolver, a machete but looked more like a short sword, then handed him a charm made of sticks weaved together to make a oval shape that fitted in the palm of his hand he looked at Luthano quizzically.

"It's a Hag charm".

Adam was not impressed.

"How do we kill it".

"It won't be easy, there are three stages, first she will try to make you see things mess with your mind, second she will talk

and offer you wishes anything your heart desires that sort of thing".
"And the third".
"She will attack you physically, Hags are strong when out done and cornered".
"Oh so not too hard then".
Adam said sarcastically but the Fair Ones just did not get it and he just shook his head and then headed back over to dock building it was getting dark when they arrived.
Adam again felt sick and knew they were at the right spot, with the charm in his left hand the sidearm in the other, he felt nervous as he neared then out of the building came his father.
"Son what are you doing here, you know I did not want this for you".
He said Adam felt confused.
"Whatever you see ignore it".
Luthano said which helped clear Adam's head.
"Adam, quick stay back, it's dangerous in there, I've come back to help you my love".
Ithilli said. Adam pointed the sidearm at her but hesitated.
"Why would you shoot me, I love you".
She said.

"She would not say that, your tricks don't work on me Hag".
He said as they stepped inside Luthano held a lamp. It was then that Adam noticed he was going in first.
"Adam, I can give you so much, make Ithilli love you, end all of this for you, lay down your weapons".
"No Hag you can't offer me anything, unless you can help".
Adam said.
"Yes, who is the mole, and how does it end oh great one".
Luthano said seeing where Adam was going with it.
"Give yourselves to me and all knowledge will be yours".
Her voice was smooth and sensuous.
"At least sweeten the deal here, give us something".
"The answers you seek are where the fallen dwell in the Hollow".
She said as two huge arms came out of the dark warehouse, one backhanded Luthano, he flow across the room into boxes and crates the lamp light up the hideous creature for a couple of seconds, the other

hand grabbed Adam and dragged him in towards her, she was fat and bloated sat in the corner twice his size, greasy long hair, bad teeth and breath to match, he tried to struggle free then the sick rancid smell hit him.
"You are mine now".
She said.
"This is not quite what you were offering or what I imagined".
Adam said and went to his hip to find no weapon there, now with both her massive hands around his chest and began to crush him, taking his breath away and his strength. Then he saw a blur and thought he was seeing things through lack of oxygen, head spinning then heard the shot and dropped. Luthano had quickly recovered and attacked the Hag, Adam dragged himself away to the side Luthano hacked and removed the Hags head now covered in thick black blood, then it began to melt he did not know what smells worse alive or dead.
"Will the spell on George drop now".
Adam said dusting himself off.

"Yes it will happen right away, he might not know where he is or what he may have said or done, and a headache".
Luthano said and they headed back to the Mayor's house and met by two more guards who let them in right away much to their relief.

They were safely back inside where they were to wait till it was light and once they were rested a meeting was called a very tired looking George who apologised and thanked Adam and Luthano for understanding. they were to go to the train station where the zeppelins were kept but it would mean leaving the safety of the walls to reach the last aircraft. Adam had Sarah, Richard, Preach and two of George's men were to go as one was to pilot and the key to reach the zeppelin shed it could be seen above the dome of the station it but before them was a sea of Fainters wondering around.
"We should use a Walkermotive to carry us across them".
Adam suggested.

"And a diversion could help to".
Richard added, they all gathered what would be needed such as food, ammo, weapons and the explosions their suits too. Then it was decided the five headed would head over to Micklegate Bar so they could use the portcullis they used the Walkermotive, Richard would drive and carry them two at a time to the station. Adam and Sarah moved further down the battlement and made noise and throw items to distract the fainters, while the portcullis was quickly lifted then took the machine through and closed it again they were to lower themselves from the wall to the steam vehicle, it was a slow process but worked the Fainters were just push aside and did not agitate them with it been dark to and their behaviour changed at night they seemed quieter and settled, George had captured one and observed it they were almost Rabid their minds gone but they were not zombies as they had first thought but they passed on a virus a corruption of some kind through a bite or bodily fluid, which made them dangerous and angry,

First Richard went and the pilot so they could get the thing warmed up and fuelled ready for them, it took three trips there were a few Fainters in the station and on the platform but could be easily avoided they made their way through to the other side to where the high platform had to be climbed up to where the Zeppelin was docket where the two sets of router blades slowly spun on either side of the cockpit and back compartment that were suspended below the massive frame where grey cloth was starched over they entered it was big and nicely furnished only the rich used them but it did not matter now in the centre sat barrels of the explosives this was not a sightseeing holiday they unhooked it and slowly rose up once clear the router blade were turned up to full power and they headed out they could not see much blow them and it was a very clear and cool night the smog had all but gone now that the factories stood silent and the chimneys no longer belched out black smoke causing pollution they looked at Adam who was not enjoying it one bit it made him feel sick and

when the wind rocked it he had to hold on
and felt very nervous and did not want to
look at the view either this made the others
laugh Adam spoke to Sarah trying to take
his mind off it she looked troubled.
"I do love him Adam, but it's hard with him
been a Fair one now and his memories, he
is very busy too".
She said speaking first.
"Give him time, he has had a lot happen to
him in such a short time, with more and
more pressure, maybe after this is over".
Adam said trying to sound positive but he
could not see this been resolved anytime
soon or a good outcome he had gone from
been a simple constable just getting by now
he was fighting supernatural monsters and
demons from stories and myths were now
very real looking back if he had told
somebody about it they would think him
crazy now it seemed like an everyday thing.
"Thanks Adam, I realised how selfish I was
being, I've spent far too much time alone,
shunned for being different and called
crazy".
She said.
"I think this whole situation is crazy".

The two laughed then they all decided to get some rest, the journey would take a couple of days, the pilots worked the coordinates out given to them by George, the rooms were luxurious with red velvet curtains with golden trims, leather chairs and seating, Adam found it hard to sleep with the rocking and the engine humming so read the books on the mythical place, the different artists impressions, he did not believe it, most thought the Earth was flat never mind hollow. He awoke early after managing to sleep a little, he could smell bacon and entered the dining area to find breakfast waiting his stomach rumbling, Preacher and Richard were already took in he grabbed the full English breakfast with tea then Sarah joined them. After eating and feeling very full having not eaten this well in a long time, the airship was well stocked, they looked at the wonderful view of the English countryside, Adam took a quick look but was not so sure. They chatted making small talk, it gave them time to relax and rest after all that had happened.

*

Ithilli and Tom watched as the portal closed, now destroyed the shamans died as it backfired and what was left of the army of the Wrong just wondered about without a leader not even noticing the two they quickly left, Ithilli decided to pay the Dryad a visit they were not attacked either she was waiting as if expecting them.
"You have done well, Now the Founders or Ancients as you know them won't have as big an army now, they have many of which they will turn against you and your world, but I have felt a Fair one of power has returned and was there with you the whole time I once loved him we created so much, he was the dweller and now with his mind returned he is the mighty Luthano".
She said, Ithilli of course knew of him and met him as the Dweller but weather this was a good thing or not was yet to be seen.
"I want some answers from you and the truth; you might still be able to fix this mess".
Ithilli said it was more like a demand she meant business having been put through all

of this she hoped Adam and the others
were ok, the Dryad still had power and was
not yet totally corrupted.

"It would be better if I showed you from the
beginning and what was meant to be".

As soon as the Dryad spoke images entered
their minds, a people who stood tall with
slim bodies and long necks large heads with
big eyes, waring smooth tight fitting
material they saw an advanced civilisation
tall towers of stone and glass they knew
how to manipulate the world around them
they built vast cities all over the wold each
linked in in a style or way such as pyramids
and ziggurats they worshipped gods they
had science and maths, using electricity to
light and power the cities, but they also
went beyond this finding other realms and
worlds they gained vast power but even
that was not enough to save them from
themselves this power began to twist and
corrupt over stretching them until the
world changed this for them the climate
changed floods and the world they knew
began to change around them they had to
abandoned their cities running to other
realms and worlds but those that remained

went underground it had been an idea they had toss around for a while but in the end they were forced to do so only a shadow of them remained on the Earth's surface hints of a great past, so the Founders created the Hollow Earth and took with them their knowledge, the world above them changed to the present day the people left with only guesses and clues to what went before them a broken legacy, but in their underworld they grew bitter and hated the top Dwellers they killed one another stole and hated abused their planet, so the Fair Ones were created by mating with human females the only good that was left of the Founders bringing with them technology to help the humans as they called them but the Founders grew tired of the Hollow and wanted back their world their surface and were not happy they did not have the power they once had they too had lost their ancient knowledge with their own puzzle pieces and so could not do this on their own so they tapped into the realms and world but there was one that remained allusive a dark realm and they found a way to access this place that promised so much yet it infected them and it did not take much to push them over the edge they began infecting the places around them the different worlds and realm fell before them until only two remained the Fair Realm they too were once peaceful but the dark infection and corruption seeped its way in turning them against themselves until one rose among them a great leader one they had placed there themselves a harbinger but something went wrong he was supposed to destroy, Tom and Ithilli saw a battle like no other it raged for months and would not unite but he did, the founders worked among them in secret and managed to get the one called Luthano exiled to Earth their former world and home then he could be used again he would pave the way and had now rose again and gain his former glory and strength test him and corrupt him because of the things he had done the guilt would eat him up in side so they could use him as their tool once again.

Tom and Ithilli looked at each other both knowing they had to return to the human realm and warn them of what was coming she took it all in but Tom struggled with it and so had questions with it all been too much to take in at once.

"So the founders want back in and have been using some dark power to regain their former power, because they are so messed up and want to use that Dweller chap to lead the Wrong, am I with it so far".
He said.

"Yes that about sums it up, and we need to get back to Earth too".
Ithilli said to Tom and directed it at the Dryad to

"Marlitho is the one responsible she brought the Founders through the Hollow it had also been their prison, the ancient Fair Ones fought them before they battled as a mighty flood came, only a few of the Founders survived that day and many Fair lost their lives too their city sunk beneath the waves, it is such a shame that the Founders vast knowledge could have been use for good, they thought themselves better and above and it was their undoing".
The Dryad said.

"You have also been used in this, look what evil you have caused in making the Wrong".

Ithilli said.
"I know I was blind by hate they exploited my weakness feeding my hate and resentment".
She said and sat down on a large root at the base of the massive oak the branch lifted to meet her bare buttocks.
"So how are the Founders doing this, bringing out creatures of myth and nightmare, how are they influencing others and contacting this Marlitho".
Tom asked still trying to take it all in.
"I believe it is called a mirror of manifestation a window into the darkness first they used it for good reaching out to other worlds and realms they could even travel through it".
The Dryad said.
"And if Marlitho has one, they will do the same to her as they did to you, pray on her love for Luthano, manipulate her too".
Ithilli said as they were talking she noticed the Wrong were surrounding them and she went for her sword but the Dryad held up her hand to stop her.
"Don't be alarmed by them they will not attack in fact they would more likely follow

or even fight for you, I am weak and have no influence over them now".
The Dryad said Tom was nervous and stood closer to Ithilli.
"We need to leave now and find a portal if there is any left".
She said.
"I can lead you to one and if you let me I can let you see what is happening on the Earth realm and the Hollow Earth too".
The dryad said Ithilli nodded and like before she showed them in their minds the City of York with its walls and the Fainters surrounding it the birds and Harpies it did not look good. And the Dweller too who now they knew him as Luthano.
"He has his memories back now and the Fair Ones follow him, I can't find Marlitho she is blocking me somehow".
She said.
"What the hell is surrounding them they look like those people are sleep walking or something".
Tom said.
"Marlitho's work she will more than likely have a human helping her too, she has been using that mirror and has infected their

minds, but the more she uses it for evil the more it will transform her and will slowly become the Wrong, she may not know the full consequences of what she is doing, and is more likely blinded by it too".

The Dryad said it was getting dark now and Ithilli felt tried their search for a way back would have to wait she hoped Adam was alright a lot had happened since they had been away and she wished she had not left but it had not been a wasted trip, the Dryad let them stay with her the Wrong backed away so they could make a fire sleep and be safe for the night.

Chapter 9

George awoke early to shouting and panic so he looked out of his window where cleared streets had been now there stood the Fainters that had somehow broken in through the night the harpies shrieked overhead bad things seemed to always happen when Adam left he thought, it had been hard work getting the Fainters out the first time it had to of been an inside job, but who and why maybe the Fair Ones, but they were loyal to Luthano, he shook his head they seemed to be fight an uphill battle and he missed Jillith more than ever she would of known what to do, the last month had been hard and stressful he was tired and missed working in his workshop inventing

and tinkering now he was fighting hordes of sleepwalking people who were close to been zombies well apart from the undead part that's what they might as well be though, then something strange had the Fainters parted and a Fair One female walked through them untouched and looking very pleased with herself. Luthano came into the office and looked out.
"It's Marlitho, it's about time she showed up".
Luthano said.
"Yes and it's all going to plan".
Said a man who entered the room as well George only knew him as Edward and another wearing the armour suit, he had been very helpful and willing then it hit him the very man helping build the walls was the one letting them in again he was holding a shotgun and pointed it at them.
"She will see you now gentlemen, the Fainters won't touch or hurt you yet".
He said and pointed with the weapon for them to go first they walked outside there was a strange silence.
"You will regret this Ed, she is only using you, she is good at that, then you will be

pushed aside and thrown in the trash, or become one of them".
Luthano said.
"We will see about that".
Edward said as Marlitho stepped forward to meet them she was smiling but she looked different to most Fair Ones not so beautiful or slender with dark round her eyes lumps and bumps and muscles, clawed fingers.
"I see you are back with followers but no army, surrender now and join me you won't become like the rest".
She said.
"I will never join you or love you Marlitho, you are under a dark influence and a fool to think the Founders will let you join them, they are using you".
Luthano said defiantly.
"We will see about that".
She said then looked at George.
"And you have been a thorn in my side. Edward lock him up".
She said and he pointed the shot gun at him.
"Ok Marlitho let them all go it's me you want, I will come".

He said holding his hands up in a surrendering way she just laughed.
"If only it was that easy, I will break you and these humans, once they see how much they need me and will beg for me to help them".
She said.
"You are deluded Marlitho they will push you aside rather then be at their side, you can have me but let these others go and release the Fainters from their living hell".
Luthano said demanding her to do it but it came out more of a beg then he had wanted but would do that if he had to and so they were all taken away to the prisons but separate from George, the city's defensives were now wide open.

*

They lowered the rope ladder down from the dirigible Gondola they had stopped short of the Hollows entrance and would go the rest on foot, first to scout it out then would return for the explosives not knowing how much they would need and it was sketchy at best plan wise but Adam Watts had worked with less and it was good having solid ground under feet again the terrain was easy going Moore land with the odd bush here and there it was early morning and still cold dew wet their shoes and boots, the mood between them sombre even Richard was quiet which was just not like him, they found a large mound almost a hill with stones and large round in shape boulders three of which were three or more meters high stood in such a way to form a v shape and made to look natural it was the right spot though Adam stepped in and found a rough tunnel that lead down but at the right angle to walk and just the right height if not taller it would be perfect for laying down the explosives with no way of digging out or clearing it and the further down the better, he was curious what was down here it had been all George talked about he put it out of his mind they had a job to do but if it was true then there could be so much to learn from them but if they were evil they would only make things worse if that was at all possible, he headed back to the surface but on reaching it he

found they were not alone but surrounded by four tall suited people but what they were wearing was not bulky armour it looked almost cloth like instead of segmented metal the weapons too looked light, a cross bow and spear which was what they were pointing at the four, the pilot had stayed with the dirigible and told to leave if they did not return or if something happened. One approached and to Adam looked like a female the suit was tight she had wide hips and the suit allowed for her ample breasts Adam had to stop staring at this point as to the point of her spear not far from his face, he held up his hands and the others did the same then their weapons were taken.
"We of the Hollow do not take kind to trespassers, what is your business here".
Her voice was much like that of a woman confirming his suspicions.
"We wish to speak with your leader, we are all in great danger, and we have heard stories of your existence".
Adam lied.
"How did you find this entrance".
"The Fair Ones are helping us".

"And what makes you think we would help you".
She said looking at them all, but they had worked together long enough to go along with him.
"From what we heard, you are advanced in many ways and could be our only way to survive".
Adam said but did not want to push them to far. Then the four were lead point first to the stones but the top stone was round and the ground shook the middle section of it moved down to reveal that it was a fake entrance they all stood on the ground it vibrated underfoot a platform appeared it rumbled under their feet and began to slowly lower taking them deep into the earth like a huge stone elevator and it just kept going down and picked up speed, the smooth stone walls zipped past them, it looked very dangerous and looked like it should have a guard rail he felt sick looking at the wall and it made him sway so looked down at his feet instead there was an awkward silence none knew what to say, Sarah sat cross legged the four seemed unaffected and just stood motionless.

"How much further down is it".
Adam said trying to pass the time, but they just ignored him, it took twenty minutes till it came to a stop which was just after his watch stopped working they were lead through a smooth stone cut corridor and out of that it opened up into a massive cavern the ceiling was way up and a huge city could be seen with high square towers carved out of the walls hundreds of feet high, pathways linked them with smaller squat building but what dominated the place was a massive tower suspended above a steaming pit, huge chains its links taller than a person held it in place. There were pipes everywhere, street lamps that glowed with wide paved roads and paths all clean and tidy not littered nor was there smog it was warm and humid though, all looked very neat as if designed not just mushed together or leaning over the path or roads, no washing lines it was all very quiet though no children played no laughter or talking there were small wagon type vehicles Adam could not make out what was powering them though, the leader of their capturers saw him looking.

"They are electrically powered and steam from the magma below us; we cannot pollute our air down here like you do with your air on the surface".

She said which made sense to him only the rich had electric lights in their lavish homes she lead them on he was looking at the pipes on the walls and the lamps.

"We also use thermal power and steam but not using massive smoking machines but the magma flows that are beneath use, bio lamination gives us light we are totally self-reliant and have been for centuries, so now back to you, why are you really here".

She said and Adam knew she could see through his lie they were taken to a square two story building it had small windows and looked very secure two of their escorts stood outside while the one who spoke to him and the other entered they were taken to a cell where the pilot sat which meant they had lost the dirigible but she did not lock them in but instead took off her helmet, her face beneath was not human it had a triangle shape thick lips large yellow

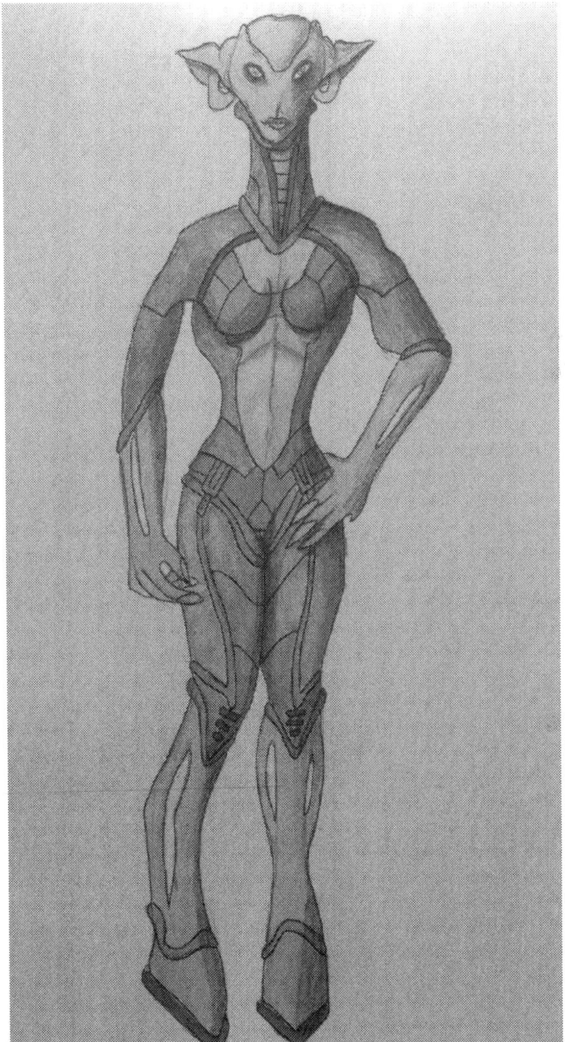

eyes with lashes' to match the rest of her face was smooth no nose just small slits where nostrils should have been and a long neck her ears pointed like the fair Ones but bigger and pointed out she seemed to be calm her face was not evil or nasty face, in fact quite pretty in a cute sort of way he found himself thinking.

"You are from the city called York what is your real purpose, don't lie to me again".
She said in a stern voice, Adam looked at the others who did not look happy, then back to her.

"We seek to destroy the entrance and there for stop the beasts you lot keep sending at us, and to study why, our leader is very keen to learn about the hollow Earth theory and he was right about this place which was thought to be a myth".

Adam said, it looked like she was about to laugh.

"Seriously that's why you are here, plus you are way off, you are a very confidant human I'll give you that".

She said then Adam smiled.

"So why did you let us in if you suspected me".

"You are one lucky and ballsy human, and it was a nice bluff, but it is a good job that I actually wanted you here, I knew as soon as you spoke, and I am well aware of what is going on, if you had not met me you would have been dead".

She said.

"So why aren't we dead, what use are we to you".

Sarah said.

"I believe we could help each other my masters the Ancient's are the ones responsible for all of this we are just caretakers and the founders, which is just a fancy title for a slave, the ancients are going to march on your world, and we don't want this to happen".

She said then Sarah punched Adam very hard on the arm, he rubbed his arm going ouch.

"That's for doing this".

Sarah said then turned back to her.

"Well thank you and don't mind him, what can we do for each other".

"My name is Ursular. York is just the beginning they will take the world and leave nothing of the old but even that is not enough there are other realms they which to take over and are infected and corrupt, you have the Fair Ones who are very powerful and the Harbinger".

Ursular said it was Sarah who knew right away she was talking about Luthano who was turning out to be very important to many people.

"I've been to the fair realm and lost friend's there it is in a bad way it's people have been kick out of their own homes or turned into the Wrong and used and so for our sake and these other places we should then work together".

Adam said.

"Who is this leader of yours you speak highly of, I would very much like to meet him".

Adam could not help but smile at what she said.

"He is a very humble man, brash and loud a crazy inventor but we would not be here if not for him, he even has a safety lamp named after him and its people where he comes from to, a Geordie is the name well so I've been told".

Adam went on to tell her of his obsession with the Hollow Earth the other inventions. "I have studied the humans and have great fondness, there are a growing number of us that want to break away from the Ancient ones, I will help you escape but those loyal to them are already marching on York, paving the way for the Ancient".
Ursular said.
"So you will help us".
Adam said she nodded.
"We have a means of great distance travel using a device called a manifestation mirror, you stand in front of it think where you want to go or a person and it will take you straight to them, but we must get to the great tower where it is kept, as for blowing up the entrance to stop the Folklore beasts, it's the mirrors that let them through, it would have been a mole, someone on the inside letting them through".
She said and the four could only agree with nothing to lose now that they had failed the mission and blowing up the entrance would not have done any good.
"I will return at the night cycle, you can trust me".

With that she left and they were locked in it gave them time to rest and drink the water left for them and food.

"So George was right about this place, he would love it".

The Preacher said and they all agreed, they were all used to everything being big, oil, smoky and loud. The materials here seemed thinner, pipes were smaller, it was clean, neat and tidy. The buildings too had smooth walls, there was no timber, the stone fitted together with no mortar a thin blade could not be pushed in between, no rough edges, the floors were the same with symmetrical patterns. The room/cell only had two beds they let Sarah take one, the other bed they played, rock, paper and scissors and took it in turns.

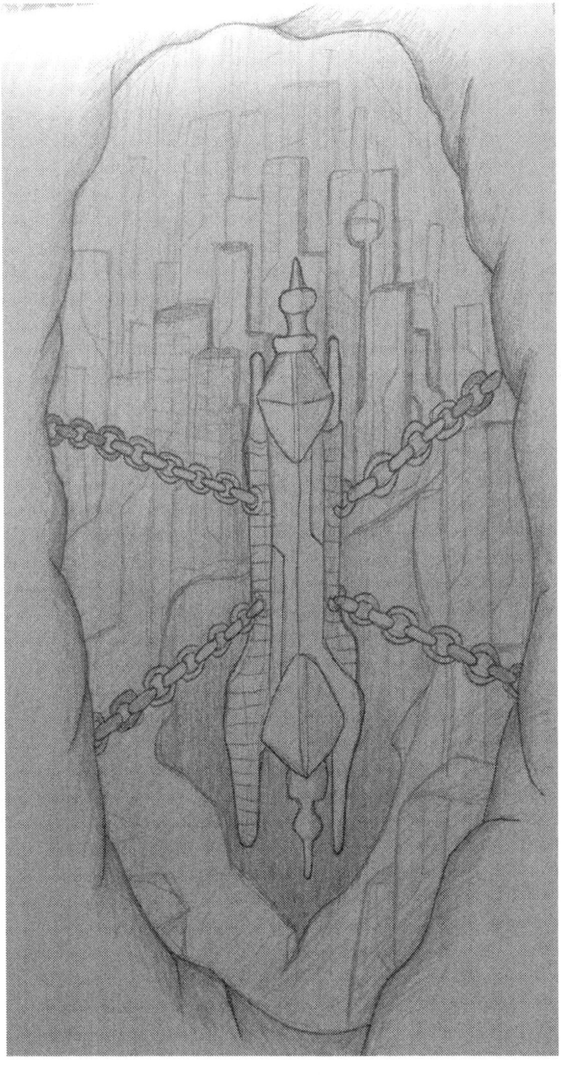

Ursular returned a few hours later but did not look happy.

"We must leave quickly, I have a safe house not far from here, my sympathisers will turn a blind eye to having surface dwellers here, and there is another human I want you to meet".

She said and hurried out keeping them to side streets and alleyways, there were no smelly alleys, rubbish or the homeless, no poor district. She took them to one of the many bridges and walkways that were very high up, it lead them to the elaborate tower blocks that were carved out of the walls, with complex paths that seemed to defy gravity, the buildings were staggered and stepped but not just one layer but several with more roads and pathways between them, all this hundreds of meters in the air and below that a massive crevasse, a dark pit of unknown depths.

She lead them into the high labyrinth of which the humans would have become helplessly lost by now, this tower block looked older and out of the way off a beaten track, she kept looking around nervously, hurrying them along and keeping them together, they entered the block, the air was cool inside, but instead of heading up she took them down smooth carved stairs then through a heavy door, inside it was furnished with thick carpets, wall hangings depicting strange scenes, huge luxurious sofas and chairs made from some unknown material that shone and glittered, but what drew their attention was an old bearded man sat at a desk full of papers and scrolls.

"Enoch you have guests who we need to hide for a while".

She said and he put down his quill and turned to them.

"Welcome brothers and sister, it's been some time since I have spoken to my own kin, these Folk are kind enough, and there is much to see, but for now rest and I will try to answer your questions and you must have many".

He said in a firm but kind tone, they sat and were brought food which was dried fruit and water too. Ursular left them saying she would return as soon as possible.

It was Preacher who approached the old man first, but he hesitated not knowing where to start.

"Are you thee Enoch as in Noah's great grandfather the seventh son".

Matthew blurted it all out not taking a breath he wished Lucy could have been with him.

"I don't claim to be those I'm just an old man that has lived more than any mortal should have, and seen far too much".

He said reluctantly.

"The book of Enoch, the accounts in there that match what is happening again, is including Giants".

"What book are you referring too, I have scrolls that I have written in Aramaic, some of my works may have been seen, if there is a book it's fake."

Enoch said and did not seem impressed.

"Many claim to have read your work and translated it and caused quite a stir with the church including a cult called the Elect".

Matthew said.

"This is strange, they are early accounts from what I have seen and were shown by the people that brought you here, who I

have lived among, they showed me kindness, but there is unrest in their ranks a corruption it has become unsafe even for me as their guest here".
Enoch said.
"Will you help us, the events match some of what you said to have written or witnessed, what can you tell us of the Hollow Earth dwellers".
"It would be better if I showed you young man, and then we can work to get my side of this put right, it seems my work has been changed, twisted, misused and misinterpreted".
"It would be an honour to work with th....".
"Stop calling me thee, I'm just a man, you folk need to rest".
With that said he went back to writing again, Matthew joined the others ate and sat with them, but he found it hard to concentrate to have met an actual person mentioned in the bible if only a little, and over two thousand years old, it was far too much information to process, the others were not so star struck.

After eating and relaxing Enoch came and gathered them all, ready to listen to him, he looked thin and frail but firm of mind and command when he spoke.
"I'm just as much a human as yourselves when they came for me, they were angelic and magical, I was a simple sheep herder, I don't know why they chose me, through my mind they showed me impossible things how they had first came to man, showed and gave them knowledge and even mixed their seed with them, but great evil made them turn on each other, they fought in a huge battle with waves of soldiers clashing and crashing, it raged for days until they were all but drowning in bodies, only a hand full escaped to live on and start the human race afresh but much was lost, only fragments remain from those great days, the Hollow dwellers went their separate ways the others spread out into the world, you have seen the pyramids and ziggurats parts of a civilization now lost in time, the builders gone."
He said and let it settle in.
"I was also shown other worlds that are parallel with your own, in some cases all but

merged, a Vale is all that stands between these worlds and it is weak, the Hollow Ones decided to start again, to try and reclaim what was lost, they travelled these worlds and took me with them using the tower of mirrors, you have seen it suspended above the great darkness".
He took a sip of water.

"So I guess the Fair Ones were created and came to us in the hopes of not making the same mistakes, but evil and corruption walks amongst them, we have seen it".
Adam said showing Enoch the lens.

"And there is more, I have seen insects infecting people they exist simultaneously with in our world or plane and these could be the reason behind it all".

"You could be right, but I've not encountered such a thing before, but worth investigating, how does this lens work".

"A friend of ours, he's a good man called George invented it and the first to see the demons, we have been fighting them and their evil influence".

Matthew said then filled the old man in of the past events, then of Lucy and H J Longsfield the Elect leader.

"Her discoverers are very close in deed, I will show you".

Enoch said and the ancient man did not seem at all phased by what they had just told him. They left Richard and the pilot Adam, Sarah and the Preacher followed Enoch, once outside he set a strong fast pace.

"When did these people first approach you".

Matthew asked keeping up with him.

"I really couldn't tell you, maybe it was just random or they saw something special, a bright light awoke me in one night she was like an angel, Ursular brought me here, I could not read or write or knew much of world beyond the fields and my flock, they showed me such wonders, I learned not just one language but them all, I read sacred books and texts that contain vast knowledge that were long ago burned and lost, they showed me the past present and what could be our future, Earth has to change its ways, my time has come the world will know, these people only want to share their knowledge the Fair Ones were the way, and this evil is not their fault".

Enoch said and took them on a long walk
through narrow streets and roads then
came to a tunnel here he stopped.

"We will be entering the dark territories,
stick together if you become separate or
lost you will be done for, not even these will
people enter here without weapons or
along, there are all manner of creatures, all
very hungry".

He said then opened a small wooden door
covered in dust and dirt, they would have
missed it, and had to crouch down to enter,
once inside the tunnel was pitch black, tall
enough to stand the air cool, Enoch lit a
torch and gave them one each, once all
were burning he once more lead the way,
the walls were not as smooth here, it was
not long before they came out into a vast
chamber, the cave ceiling seemed hundreds
of meters above them where veins of the
luminous substance could be made out,
Adam stepped back in surprise as
something brushed passed his leg but on
shining his torch lower instantly wish he
had not, it was a massive pale spider with
enormous front legs, it went on its way
leaving him with a shudder and wish he had

his armour suite on. Enoch shook his head in a disapproving way and resumed his fast pace, the path he took was worn with use and slippery in places, this brought them to another tunnel, but this was smoother with steps which took them deeper still, they all walked in silence in their own thoughts.

It was a long time before Enoch stopped at a large metal door, he put out the torch but all four had to push it open and it was warm to the touch they were met by a brightly lit enormous long and high chamber along the walls were rose of stone statues each Giants stood meters tall some were different there were taller ones, muscled ones, male and female all very life like. At one end stood a huge stone throne not meant for a normal human to climb up or for that matter sit in it, everywhere there were pictures and stone carving, swirling patterns and shapes, very organic that were almost flame and smoke like in nature the throne too.
"I don't feel so great in this room, it's all moving and weird, and it's too bright as well".

Sarah said they told Enoch of her ability and he quickly took them from the room, once back in the cave corridor she soon felt better.

"What did you see in the young lady". Enoch asked.

"It was like all the pictures and sculptures were moving as if real, it hurt my mind to look upon it all, like feeling it and seeing it". She said feeling weak, they headed back the old man did not speak for a long time.

"I believe you saw the Lord of the spirits throne".

"Who, I don't understand".

"He means God Sarah".

Preacher said and they all looked at him.

"I have seen this vision also, there are many realms but none so bright as his, the Giants were being judged by the almighty".

"This is all turning a little too religious for my liking".

"Have you not witnessed greatness, magic and miracles all around you. These are the early days not what your religion depict now, even before the messiah was born, there are other Gods too, I have seen them all in their glory, my mind has been opened to all the possibilities, we have one more stop".

Enoch said and lead the way once more but took a different path and stopped at another metal door this was cold to the touch as they all once more pushed this one but he stopped them so there was a small gap to see into the chamber beyond it was just as vast as the last one if not bigger, here there were row upon row of Hollow Dwellers all knelt silently as if in prayer, then they saw who or it they were kneeling before, it was a stone Giant, but this was different it was huge and deformed like the Wrong, all out of proportion this was no statue, it moved and was not alone, there were more. It was Sarah again that pulled back with a sharp intake of breath, then she got them all to use the lens, and shared with Enoch, the whole room was swarming with the bugs. They all got away and back to the Hollow as fast as possible and back to Enoch's room where Ursula was waiting and she did not look happy at all.

from Enoch's room with her guards they walked them through the streets the lighting outside was a lot dimmer than before and the streets were empty none stopped them as they headed to the tower which was very tall and angular as high as the York minster and just as impressive hanging above a hole suspended by the chains.

"We will have to climb using the chain maintenance ladders, they won't drop the drawbridge for me anymore".

Ursula said as they approached the chain housing just one link was the size of a one story house making them feel very small compared to the all but alien architecture, this chain had feet and hand rails Ursula lead the way, Preacher Matthew looked at Enoch who he could see was not going with them.

"Go, we will meet again if not in this life or realm but the next, there is much still to learn".

The old man said Matthew nodded and climbed after the others. It was not an easy climb about halfway it grew very hot making them sweat leaving damp patches on their clothes, here the metal was hot, the suspended tower seemed to grow bigger as they slowly approached it, they kept seeing more and more of the black bugs but not where it was hot, they reached the tower and climbed from the last link, Adam looked down and cursed himself for doing it all the time, the drop made his head spin, the tower was made of metal not stone like the rest. Ursula took them along a narrow ledge, which they had to put their backs to the wall and shuffle along, she stopped at a window and disappeared inside then a moment later she reached down and began helping them all right inside.

The walls were shiny with smooth tiles on the ground with strange organic statues, she took them up inside an elevator it was nothing like their big metal ones with a simple button press it went up and quite fast it pulled at their stomachs a little the doors swished open smoothly at the top Ursular spoke in a strange language to the guards who let her through without question which showed her high position when they were away from the guard she told them they were to be executed and is

one of the uses of the mirrors which to
Adam did not fill him with any enthusiasm
to step through one of them, she took them
to a huge chamber at the towers top in the
centre was a framework with many mirrors
but they were not like Adam expected them
to be they were oblong and two meters tall
but they were not glass like a normal one
they were shiny the reflection was very dull
and distorted she told them to stand in
front of one each and asked them where
they desired on George's office in the
mayor's house the image of the room came
up but clear they all had to think and
concentrate too then step forward Adam
felt sick as he stepped through the image
changed and twisted around him then he
found himself on his knees facing the other
way in the office the others stood round
him and laughed, he could not believe it
had just happen and was so easy. But the
office was empty as was the rest of the
building so they thought at first then they
found the young man called Edward he was
very afraid and told them that an army had
arrived surrounding the walls and the
fainters were now inside the walls and that

George and Luthano were Marlitho the Fair one's prisoners now and had easily overtaken them.

"Marlitho has a mirror and is very evil, she will have let them through, but they are only using her you will all be slaves as we are to the rock skins".

Ursular said,

"They are been held in Clifford's Tower, I saw them taken I feel ashamed for hiding". Edward said.

"No you did right, take us once it is dark, and tell us anything that might help". Adam said reassuring him, they stayed hidden waiting till nightfall Edward told them that they were all taken prisoner and that they had appeared inside the walls and that they had not stood a chance against them they told Edward that the plan had failed but some of the founders were not evil as the ones who took the city and to trust her and also that the Ancients were going to enslave them all and that Luthano was special, Edward agreed to take them he showed them a back way out of the house through a hidden door in the cellar which brought them out on a small door beside the river where small boats were moored which they took out onto the dark choppy water keeping to the side moving slowly so as not to be noticed too easily and a quicker way to reach the Skeldergate bridge where they hid the boats and went on foot to the tower that stood on the steep hill that it sat on heading to the stairs, but as they reached it they were then surrounded by the founder soldiers and torches spears pointing right at them but not Edward he stood back as the Fair one called Marlitho approached them he stood beside her smiling and the now five realised they had just been had, their weapons were removed and they were taken and put in a cell beside George and Richard, where Ursular was introduced to him, the inventor told them Luthano was not there but the rest they already knew.

"Wow I have you all together, all the thorns in my side right here".

Marlitho said. Then a huge Founder male came over she looked at Ursular and said.

"And a defector to".

"Yes we have known about them".

He said.

"Arbrac you are just sore because not only did I turn you down but my group did to". Ursular said then added.

"You are all fools do you think they will let you be at their side the Ancients don't care were all just slaves to them cattle even, York will fall first then the world will be next".

"Well you will be the first to fall so the world can be reborn a fresh start and if I have to die for this to happen so be it". Marlitho said and walked away.

"I wish Luthano was here he would know what to do, I Guess this is it".
Sarah said.

"No we aren't done yet, Ursular tell me more about the Ancients".
George said.

"There are many throughout this world and the known realms, most lay dormant or don't care for the matters of man and Fair ones, but for some reason the stone skins are very much awake but corrupt, a sickness has taken over them, Marlitho has it too and those loyal to the Rock skins, and your own kind, the Fainters".
She said.

"Could a bug be responsible I saw remains and I'm no expert, but they were big and nothing I've seen before we just thought they came with the Fair ones".
Adam said.
"Yes I've seen them too, like I could see the corrupt ones they were hidden within the vale spell too".
Sarah said Ursular did not look happy at what the two said.
"There could be another ancient awake, pulling all our strings here, we can only wait and see how it pans out and how that hand will be dealt, right now we need to get out of here".
She said and the others agreed then she turned to George.
"I know you lead these people, and I'm sorry for taking over".
"No it's fine love, we could do with a pair of fresh eyes, and yours are very pretty".
He said they all rolled their eyes and tutted but they were smiling at least, he always had a way to lighten the mood or say something witty.

"Well thank you, nobody has ever told me that, our courtship is usually armed combat".
Ursular said and she was deadly serious.
"He might wrestle you if you want".
Richard said making them laugh.
"Can we get back on track here".
Adam said but he too was trying not to laugh they tried to straighten their faces, he was right though, such things would have to wait, they took this time to rest and sat on the could stone floor.

*

Adam awoke feeling very cold and stiff and wondered what it was then he saw a guard run past leaving his post there was a lot of noise and orders been shouted and they did not look happy it was more like fear he woke the others but they too had heard the commotion and were just has confused as him and they did not tell the prisoners, then there was the sound of fighting more running around, then the door too their cells opened and a familiar face stepped out of the shadows it was Ithilli and Tom.

"You lot staying in there then".

She said with a smile, Adam wanted to rush over to her and hold her so tight he had missed her and thought her dead, George was also happy to see the two having blamed Adam for losing them he gave then a hug, Adam could see that Tom was like a son to George.

"There is much to discus, but right now I have an army of the wrong and have just taken you all by surprise".

She said then looked at Ursular they explained to her who she was and what had been happening since she had been away

and those they had lost jillith been one to the bug and fainters.
"What of Luthano and Marlitho".
Adam asked her.
"I've not seen them I was hoping you might know".
Ithilli said standing close to her he wanted to be alone with her but why would a Fair one like or ever love him either way he wanted to tell her, she lead them outside and up onto the battlements it was early morning and the bright light hurt their eyes what they saw was a dark army of misfits and monsters and they outnumbered the founders by thousands stretching out as far as the eye could see the founders who had given up on fighting such a force who would fight without fear and die for Ithilli and those who had wronged and made them this way.
"Well done Ithilli, thought you were dead lass, don't do that again to this old man".
George said clamping a big arm around her slender shoulders and looked like he might break her but Adam knew she was tougher then she looked then something strange happened the Wrong parted letting

Luthano walking towards them they went down to meet him.

"She escaped through a mirror I must stop Marlitho".

He said and he was happy to see them free and all together then looked at Ursular who was stood with George.

"I will show you how to use it, but there is little time to explain, the ancients will be on their way now that the Founders have failed and they will not be happy".

They headed back to the mayor's house where Marlitho had run to.

"I have a feeling she will be heading for the source of all of this, follow her all you have to do is think about her and you will then be able to keep up with her you have Founder blood in you so once out in the realms you won't need the mirror, get to her and close the realms it is the only way to halt the rock skins".

Ursular said.

"Well whoever you are thank you, I will do what I can, what about you all though".
Luthano said.

"We will hold them off till you are done, you are the Harbinger, when given the choice may you choose wisely, now go". She said then he turned to Sarah and embraced her then turned to the mirror and was gone, then the big founder male came to them and looked at Ithilli and bowed down to her and Ursular.
"Our lives are yours and we will help where we can if you will have us".
He said Ithilli looked at her and she nodded.
"You were always easily lead, at least you know when you are beaten, we will need all to do this and little time to prepare".
She said to them all.
"The rock skins will walk across the land five in all, all we can do is slow them and give the Harbinger time it will take all we have to do this".
Ursular said and so they would divide up George and Adam the walkermotives, Ursular her own people and Ithilli the wrong.

*

Edward was now sat in the very cell he had put George in, Marlitho had just left him with nothing, no you will rule at my side or treasure beyond measure. He sat feeling sorry for himself.
"Boy did you back the wrong horse".
Said a muffled voice behind the gas mask and armour, he removed it and unlocked the cell door.
"We can help each other friend, I'm Henry". He said and shook Edwards hand.
"What will we do".
"You have no employment or purpose, join me brother, let me show you a different guiding light. You will find eternal glory at his side, the Lord of the spirits will be your strength, you faith a shield"
He said and his words seemed to make sense to Edward. The two slipped away from the old prison.
"What is your plan".
He said.
"There is one among them who has turned his back on our Lord, and he must be punished, then we will wake the others from their sleep, then we will punish all that have stepped away from the light starting

with the Fair Ones with their serpent tongues, and let them burn".
Henry said.
"Who is this man".
"Preacher Matthew King".

Chapter 10

Once his head stopped spinning and the sickness faded he was stood on familiar ground yet it was very different, the former beauty was gone and it ached his heart to see it in such a state, gone where the lush forest once stood now the trees looked like skeletal hands reach up out of the cracked dry earth, rivers of oil like sludge he knew where he was heading he saw the mighty oak first and it too was in a bad way his heart quickened for his first love the beautiful Dryad he found her laying on the ground beneath the rotting branches she was bleeding badly Luthano knelt beside her lifting her head she moaned and half opened her green eyes as if sensing or knowing who it was.

"She did this to me but it was the old one who poisoned me her bugs have spread far and have been doing so for as far back as the first of our kind they have been hitching a ride every time we crossed over to different realms we were the ones killing and infecting, Marlitho has gone mad but she too has been under the bugs influence, the fate of us all lies in your hands it has all been leading up to this moment".

She said weakly. It looked like she had been beaten and was close to death.

"Save your strength I will return for you and put an end to this".

He said.

"No, once you leave this realm it will be sealed off forever thus weakening the Rock skins, now go".

She spoke loud and clear almost looking like her former self then she slowly died drying up like a leaf returning to the earth form once she came he knew she was at peace now he stood for a long moment dried his tears and turned away he thought of Marlitho and where she had travelled next he would have time to mourn later and take his revenge,

The sickness returned feeling like he had looped the loop and again she was one step ahead of him but leaving a trail of destruction for him to follow this realm to was sick and infected this was the place of myth and dreams where the Harpies and the succubus came from now it to was a waist land too it had high mountain and wide deep valleys, they had been made out to look bad and evil but these too were life and did not deserve the magical creatures were dying or had been transformed like the wrong, black and twisted he avoided them the best he could she was no longer in this world but he knew it would seal once he left and it was a hard thing to do but it was for the best he thought of Sarah and their world, he followed Marlitho again wondering where she would take him next this world was very different again it was a hot desert like world with pyramids and great building and structures but it too lay in ruins now a necropolis then he saw its people they were the founders they too

were slaves with their world in ruins then he saw Marlitho run into what looked like an old arena with its high walls and windows like ancient Rome back on earth their influences were everywhere, as he entered he knew it was a trap but too late a huge block of stone blocked his way out .
"Stop Luthano it's too late, there is nothing you can do here or anywhere except maybe died, be seeing you".
With that said she just disappeared a huge shadow cast over him he had to back away as a huge Founder male stood before him standing at least eight foot tall if not more but he was mutated and deformed one arm and shoulder was bigger than the other and muscular he was spotty with the dark goo on his body he was seeing this liquid more and more, the beast throw a huge fist with a massive bone like blade at Luthano who barely got out of the way, he had to roll in the rough sand as another blow was coming his way, he had to stay back knowing one hit would end him and the walls were too high and smooth to climb or jump out then he had an idea and stood at the wall then ducked as it hit the wall and damaged it a

lot but the walls were very thick and would take more hits there were wooden torches one dropped, he tried again but the beast was not stupid and not about to help him escape another punch came at him with lightning speed but the bony blade got stuck in the ground Luthano ran up the massive arm and kicked the beast in the face and got two hits in before he had to jump free as it got his fist free Luthano stayed back and did the same thing again with more kicks to the face making the black goo come out like blood, but again the beast learned he grabbed the fallen torch from moments ago it was still lit and he was about to use it as a club but the black goo on him touched the flame and was like fuel the small flame flared up it gave him an idea, the beast was coved in the stuff he just had to get close enough and he only had one chance at it he waited for an attack like before they circled each other.

"Come on show me what you got, I'm right here".

He said trying to bait it into a wrong move, it learned quick but not this time it attacked like before but did not get stuck there was only one thing he could do and that was throw it again the two weighted each other up Luthano jumped to one side then another then throw it has hard as he could the wood missed but the flame caught and it worked the goo was flammable it screamed as flame consumed it but it was not about to stop trying to get him he dodged it and the thing ran straight at the wall close to where he had punched it and caused more damage a big block was shock lose and dropped on the beast crushing its head in the sand but kept burning. Luthano climbed out he felt sorry for the thing he had to catch Marlitho and he wondered where she would take him this time one thought and he was gone another realm sealed behind him he hoped it was enough.

*

Adam marched out with a team of eight Walkermotives they moved slowly over the ground full steam weapons ready, the Wrong moved with them Ithilli stood on his machine it was so nice having her back he had not gotten any chance to speak with her yet, the dirigible over head to drop explosives then they saw them huge walking mountains of rock in a hunched over humanoid form the five towered over them even from far away they stood about five story high if not more four moved forwards, the biggest one remained behind explosives were dropped on one but had little or no effect the Wrong swamped one but it crushed them with its huge rock fists next it was the Walkermotives turn they picked one and all eight opened fire using the cannons and Gatling guns and flamethrowers when the smoke cleared it kept walking with scorch marks, bullets had only broke the surface with a few cracks here and there next th

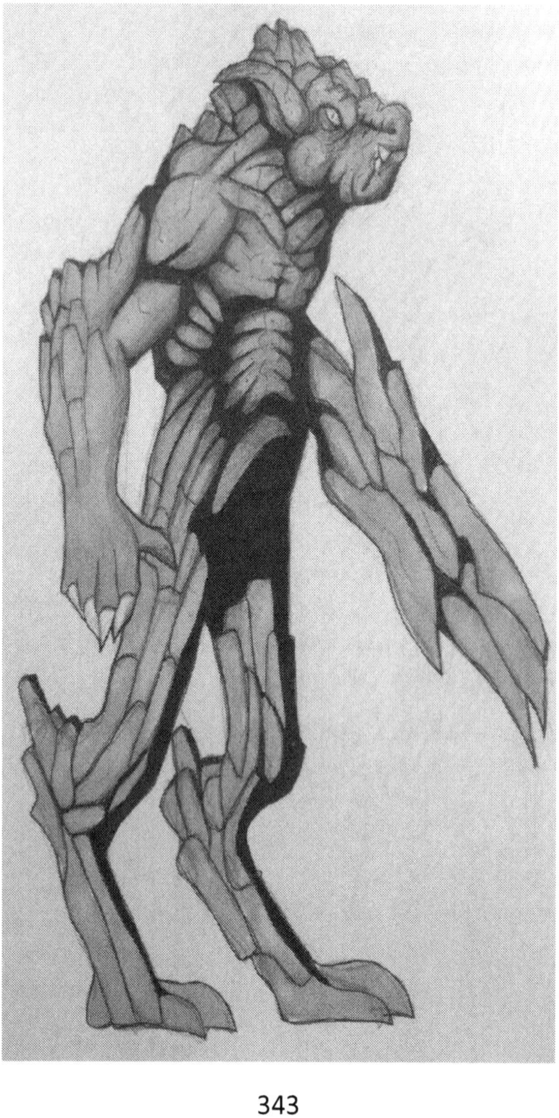

ey concentrated on just one leg and only managed to make it limp a little with all ammo used they had to pull back the Founders had been digging huge pits and traps they had camped outside the city while it was been barricaded again George over seeing everything and Ursular the two were getting very close now Adam had chance to stand with Ithilli.

"it's good having you back Illi".

He said as they rested their first wave had failed he past her a bottle of water.

"I should never have taken you, it was stupid and selfish".

She said,

"Yeah George was not best pleased, you would never have helped us with the wrong if we had not gone, thought I had lost you though".

He said. She gave him a little smile took the water and touched his hand.

"Yeah I did not think I would see you again either".

Then they had to get back to work the Rock skins moved slowly and relentlessly they all tried again but one fell but they had hardly touched it and it could mean only one thing

Luthano was succeeding but it was not quick enough the city walls were in sight they managed to stop the limping one but it took all they had then it was getting dark the three did not stop for that either the bigger one now lead the way it was the traps next one to the left of the big one fell in and got stuck in a pit full of mud they added more water now two remained they managed the last small one but the biggest was unstoppable and it reached the wall and pulled the bricks aside, they could not attack it like before with it been so close to the city all they could do now was wait for Luthano.

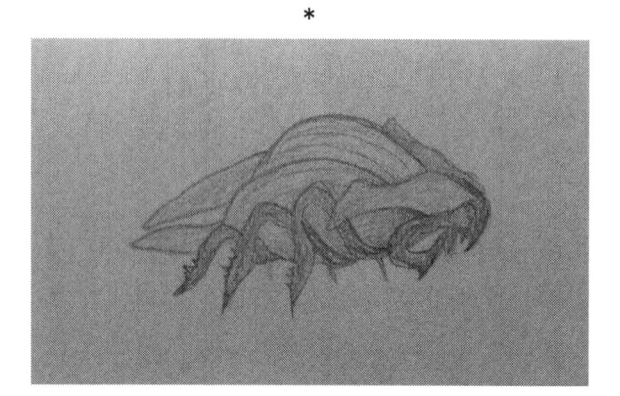

*

The land was flat and baron the sky was full of the bugs a twister of them like locusts, then in the distance he saw where they were coming from a large hill he made for it but the bugs left him alone he climbed it and made his way down inside more of the thick goo, inside it was warm and looked like a massive beehive with the worker bug were as big as a dog with pincer like mandibles again they did not go near him he climbed down deeper then reached a huge chamber it was warm the floor was squashy and gross and more goo, then stood in the centre standing on four insect legs was a female humanoid with horns and long arms and clawed hands she was big her face was pretty she was large breasted beautiful in a strange alien way, but he knew she was using the vale spell to hide her true form she stepped forward.
"Luthano Rockheart welcome, I can offer you the universe make you a god and rule at my side".
She said in a smooth voice that seemed to be in his mind at the same time and had to block her out and reached out to her mind

pushing back she was afraid of him but was trying not to.

"I'm only here for Marlitho".

He said.

"Oh I knew everything that is going on".

"That would be because you are mostly the cause, pull those bugs of yours back and I might spare you and not seal you here".

He said defiantly.

"You are talking to a goddess here, you will give me respect, I could crush you".

She said but despite her worlds he still felt fear coming from her. The organic ground parted in front of him it was Marlitho she looked pale and unconscious.

"The one who loved you is right there; my offer still stands join me".

She said softer now, Luthano looked around the chamber and saw back packs and other abandoned equipment armour and another torch the black goo was everywhere too, he knew she was the last obstacle and would not let him just walk out with Marlitho and knew her weakness.

"For me to join you, pull back from earth, all you bugs, leave the people and have me".

He said.

"You drive a hard bargain, for you yes, give me your everything mind and body and it will be done".
She said in a seductive voice now, he stepped closer and reached out to her but instead of that he rolled to the torch and back pack lit the torch and held it to the black goo.
"How about you do as I ask now, show me that you won't just consume everything and not infect all you touch". He waited for her reaction, she took a step back in surprise none had stood up to her before let alone trick her like this.
"How dare you, after I offered you the world and beyond".
"Do as I ask or burn it's that simple, then I will be yours, show me you can change, prove it now".
He said feeling confusion from her he saw all she wanted was to kill and consume, and he did not want to burn her she was ancient with such vast knowledge but she was a fake, a beast with a beautiful face, he felt anger now.
She stood on her back legs rising her front and transformed in a mixture of spider and

hideous bug creature all tentacles and claws she stomped on the

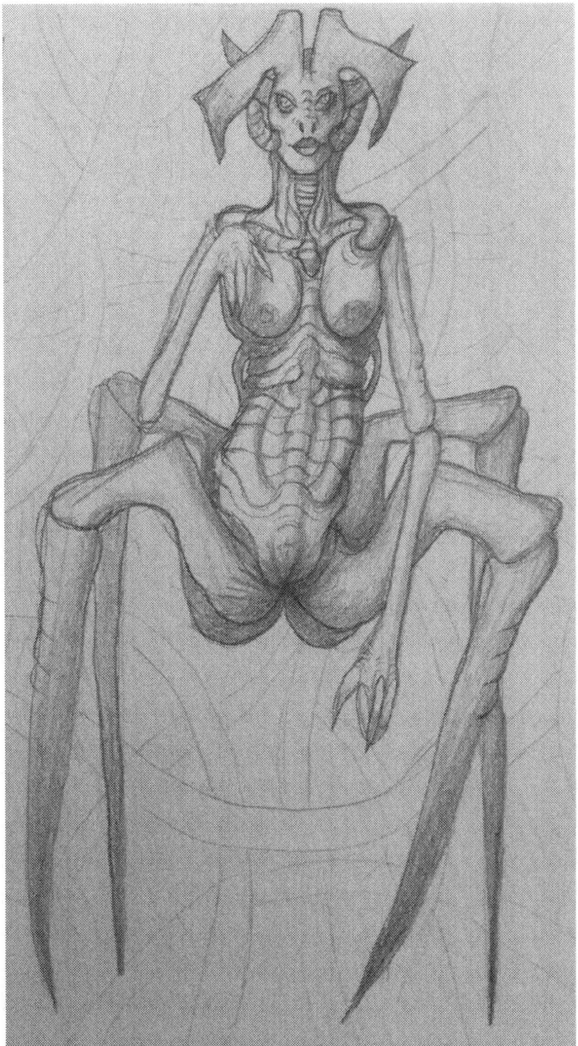

ground ground making him lose his footing and the torch he had to roll out of her way as she brought those legs which ending in evil looking spicks the torch was still lit but barely, he grabbed what he could and throw it at her then found a sword and attacked her hacking of spicks and claws as he went she/it screamed out in pain pulling back, he had made her show her true self and she was as evil on the outside as was in, he grabbed the torch and lit the goo setting the chambers walls on fire she made a hideous sound as if everything could be felt and was connected to her then the flames reach her at that point he grabbed Marlitho's body with her on his shoulder made a run for it, lighting as he went hoping to slow the queen and her massive workers it was hard going there were times he had to climb with his hands full then he had to drop the torch the whole place was up in flames now and he could feel the heat it was hard to concentrate he had to focus on Sarah and the Earth realm so he could leave but the bug hive was blocking it somehow he would have to get outside then the little ones came biting and swarming him trying to slow and stop him leaving but they could not poison him then he heard the queen in his mind screaming what she would do to him. *You will feel pain like no other, you think hell is a bad place I will make you suffer for an eternity and then some, you will burn, and I will keep you alive and do it all over again, then you will beg for death.* He shut her out and climbed onwards and was soon back outside he tried again but it was the queen stopping him, saying what she would do to him over and over, Marlitho was getting heavy he moved away from the nest and it exploded knocking him to the dry earth he lay winded but the queen was gone and out of his head he stood with Marlitho and left that place behind sealing it.

*

The Rock skin reached the walls of the city at the Monkgate Bar wall but instead of smashing through it opened its mouth and throw up laver, it burned everything it touched setting the houses on fire flowing through the streets. George had already pulled everybody back to a safe distance along Lendal bridge and crossed the water there were still a few Fair Ones even Rathan Stone who did not like common Workers or humans. But could still see the giant towering even over the Minster. Their attacks had no effect on the last big one, it was destroying everything in its path and he felt helpless even Ursular could not help and she had showed him things he never knew and he like her a lot to very much like Jillith but not which made no sense but he was liking her more and more and there was much he could learn if they survived this everybody was exhausted and had worked so very hard even the Founders but they were done, Preacher said a prayer trying his best to reassure the people, two men who were still wearing their full gear removed their helmets one was Edward the second one was not familiar to him but they were both armed but Preacher knew the one.

"It was truly sad she died, those bullets were meant for you, I will not miss this time".

Longsfield said and some of the others
turned their weapons on them too they
were the Sleepers, Peter Aldwark amongst
them, they lined them along the bridges
stone work.
"Don't do this now Henry, there is nothing
left but your want for revenge, you are a
hypocrite you say you serve the Lord of the
Spirits, you are just a fool, stand with us".
The Preacher said, Ursular was stood beside
George and held his hand.
"Edward, Peter start shooting them now
please, Matthew is mine".
Longsfield said but the two men hesitated
and looked at each other.
"Do is I order, kill them all my brothers".
They dropped their weapons even Edward,
this sent Longsfield into a rage he shouted
at them then turned on the Preacher, he
ran at him and the two men fell to the river,
the cold dark water took them under, all
watched helplessly on, they saw bubbles
then nothing.

George thought back to when this had all
started when he was just starting out back
when people laugh at him even his coal

mining father for wanting to be an inventor the long hours at night school and self-teaching did pay off even helping his father with the lamp, telling them to make the train tracks smaller and narrow, the plans for his new machine he had shown them all, life had been so care free and innocent until he had stumbled upon a dark side to it all by accident the lens and building a secret army he was watching it all go up in flames he told Ursular to stop and to leave their post there was no need to die for bricks and mortar and just as he was about to go somebody shouted it was the Preacher, he climbed out, they reached to help him back onto the bridge Richard put his big coat over his shoulders but he was alone Longsfield was lost the the undertow and the icy depths.

 And then Rock skin just stopped moving the laver went cold and when the smoke cleared Luthano was just stood there looking awesome all staring at him smoke and steam rising from him like it was nothing to have beaten the Ancients he was holding Marlitho they all went to him Sarah been the first of course.

"You have done it, you are free of the Ancients".

Ursular said he lay Marlitho down she was close to death, Rathan Stone knelt beside her, Luthano held Sarah they looked back at the body something was not right it was not over yet the body moved and he thought she was getting up but instead her belly swelled and then split open in a horrible way and out spewed the bugs he told them to get stomping and not get bitten then the body moved again jerking and twisting it began to change shifting into something big, thick bony legs poured out until it was a huge bug but not like the female or the smaller ones this was all legs spicks and horns something from a nightmare as if everybody's fears and hates had just manifested and it was full of pure rage and black goo they all pulled away but all were still in shock and felt ill and afraid at the horror they had just witnessed.

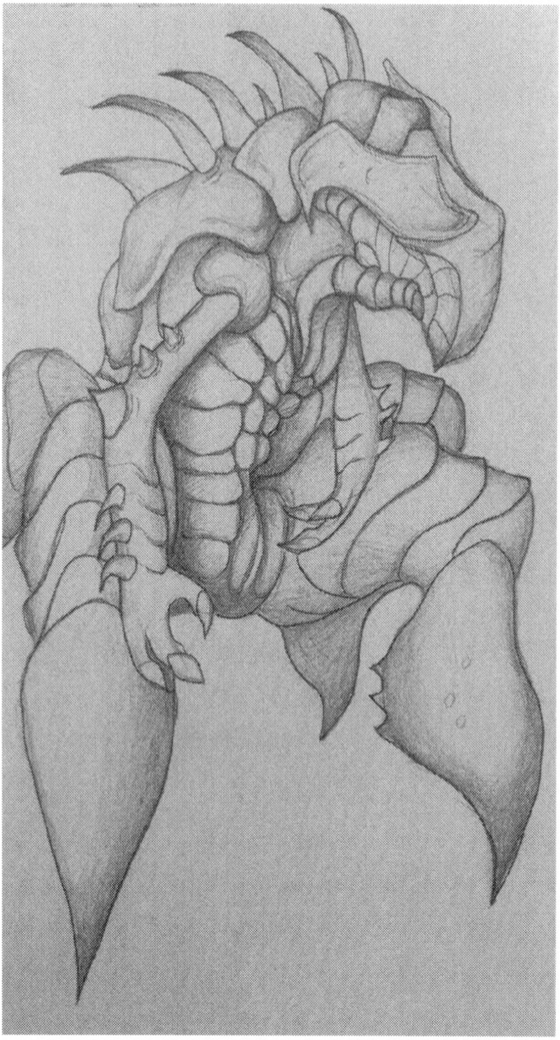

George pulled them all back but Luthano stood his ground it stamped right up to him but something had just snapped inside him he too felt hate and anger building up inside him giving him strength he felt himself change to growing bigger towering over the monster he grew two extra massive arms but what was most impressive were the wings that also grew there were six in all flowing out at different angles, and they fought hard like titans smashing each other to the ground and the very earth shook, he grabbed the insect monster and with one big updraft lifted into the air houses and buildings broke, the battle took to the sky as it grew its own set of insect wings, the two swooped down and back up again exchanging blows, tearing at each other, Luthano took the fight higher but it then had enough and was trying to escape but Luthano was not going to let that happen, he grabbed and tore its wings then the two plummeted fast to the ground and hit hard but it was Luthano who stood first as the dust settled, it was afraid like the bug queen had been, in fact he had felt this before and he did not like it, he could easily crushed the bug king but felt empty a bright light blinded him, multiple voices all speaking at once in his mind. *We are the ancient ones you have beaten the evil you can be a god at our side rule with us mighty one.*

"No I have heard this before".

He said and again felt that they were afraid of him.

"I want to go back to them to my beloved and friends, they need me, you are done, stay in the Hollow and do not interfere with the lives of mortals again, let them find their own way".

Then you would give up the power of a god to be immortal to rule over these weak beings their lives are but a blink of an eye to us.

"I will give up everything I have and my so called power, to be with them so take it all from me, leave me just as a man".

Very well this is your last chance you will be weak like them to live their short life soon to forget this.

"Yes I have lived without a past before just don't take Sarah from me".

And with that said Sarah just found him lying on the ground surrounded by the monster's body parts and goo he was weak she held him in her arms and he awoke to the warmth of her body and smiling down at him she was crying but they were tears of joy he reached up and wiped them away she helped him stand the Ancients were but a distant memory, and he had her, and she had him

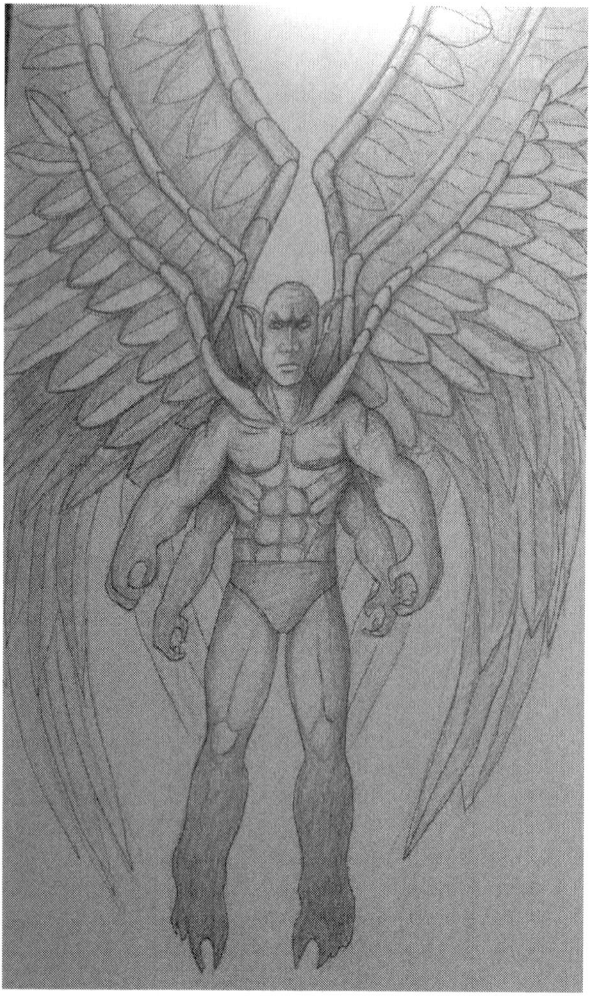

11

George with the founders help, Ithilli and Ursular had to rebuild York, mending the walls and battlements, the Fair Ones helped to but not like before they let the human folk make it on their own two feet, George took Tom on has his son and went on to make his locomotive which was to become very famous and many other inventions. The factories started up again and with it better working conditions and better homes, the machines were more efficient , Adam became the head constable and the position of justice of the peace and what had happened was hidden away, George went back with Ursular to the hollow earth learned everything from them and stayed with her too. But he kept that a secret.

*

Matthew had Lucy cremated and returned to America with her ashes and gave them to her family, he hunted the rest of the Elect, telling the followers there spiritual leader was dead and their cult was at an end, then he took up the priesthood for real knowing this was his true calling his faith stronger than ever but hid his own secrets.

The end

Printed in Poland
by Amazon Fulfillment
Poland Sp. z o.o., Wrocław